To TAMARA.

This is my greatest writing - my BABy "I have come full circle" - Through much life lessons - moves and moves and continued changes - I kept going - now my ISABELLA is complete

Love + Sparkles
Nancy Lee Amos

I truly Believe (you too) have other DREAMS - to follow - Now is The time! xoxoxo

"A new recepie to follow - A New PATH !!! ~ N.

Nre like ISABELLA and The Healing FAERIES - I BREAK Free - and SET others Free to follow Their own DREAMS & to go further

Isabella
Rules Like the Wind

Nancy Lee Amos

authorHOUSE®

AuthorHouse™
1663 Liberty Drive
Bloomington, IN 47403
www.authorhouse.com
Phone: 1-800-839-8640

First published by AuthorHouse 2/10/2011

ISBN: 978-1-4567-2728-4 (sc)
ISBN: 978-1-4567-2729-1 (e)

Printed in the United States of America

*Any people depicted in stock imagery provided
by Thinkstock are models, and such images are
being used for illustrative purposes only.
Certain stock imagery* © *Thinkstock.*

This book is printed on acid-free paper.

The FAERY TREE OF LIFE

(This <u>tree</u> is <u>in</u> the <u>original</u> Faery Garden on P.E.I.)

This Faery Wreath was hung in *our Faery Garden* on Prince Edward Island! It represents THE CIRCLE OF LIFE; with *Isabella's Scottish blue plaid scarf* and *her P.E.I. tartan plaid scarf tied together*; crisscrossing our lives together across *Oceans of Time!* The HEART SHAPED ROCK she found on the *healing shores* of Prince Edward Island symbolizes our UNIVERSAL LOVE and the small' miracles found in our everyday lives! I want to *Thank You* from the bottom of *MY HEART* for coming *full circle* with Isabella and I <u>on our journey</u>; *<u>THE JOURNEY of Healing Hearts</u>*!

v

CONTENTS

Dear Peoplefolk: Throughout this story the spelling of the word 'Fairy' has been changed to the word 'Faery' as requested by the Faeryfolk!

+ A Scottish Faery Tale +

For all you Lads and Lassies
<u>All over the world</u>
This story is for *you*...
It's all about believing
In dreams that do come true

This *is* the 'final story'
Of our *brave-heart Isabella*
With the Queen's clansmen
Standing tall and *brave* and *true*
Ready, *willing* and *able*
To watch over you!

You have to *listen carefully*
As you follow this journey through
<u>This is the *LAST TIME*</u>
The Healing Faerie's - will *reach out*
<u>So heed *their* CALL to YOU!</u>

Their message is *loud*, their message is *clear*
It's TIME to follow *your own path*
And become the leader of *your own heart*
And not in the *shadow of another's* <u>fear</u>!
So; step up, be alert, start now and *be sharp*!
<u>The TIME is drawing near</u>...

Trust in Isabella and the treasures *she holds dear*
Let yourself shine; with Joy, Peace and *Innocence*
And the gift *of KNOWING;* that dwells *inside* of you!
<u>Trust</u> - with that *childlike wonder*
That you're DREAMS *are COMING TRUE!*

MY BOOK III *is dedicated to YOU* –
   To your *Faery Faith.......*
      And to your DREAM!

****

Tis' time for the HEALING of the *world*
And the Healing *in each one* of us
<u>Believe</u> in Isabella and the HEALING FAERIES too
And know till *this day* they *still* walk among us
Know that before this day is <u>through</u>
You can change your *thoughts*, your *life*
And change those who are - *<u>surrounding YOU</u>*
By word, by thought, by deed
By a hug, a smile, a nod
Every moment, *every breath* – IS NEW
You can change *your world, your day*
<u>If only YOU BELIEVE</u>!

****

You are the *only one* who can change *YOU*
If you *stop* and <u>start again</u> – even if you think *<u>you CAN'T</u>*
YOU CAN – YOU CAN – YOU CAN!!!
For *we believe in YOU*!
You're never alone – you're always one *call* away,
One *step* away – one *room* away
TAKE that *step*; make that *call*,
Say your *thanks* <u>out loud</u>
Please be *thankful, grateful* and *full of LOVE*
And *<u>never forget</u>* your childlike
WONDER & spontaneous JOY!
And the LOVE - *<u>that ISABELLA has for you</u>*!

****

Love and Sparkles,

Nancy, the *Author* and Isabella/*Queen* of the Healing
Faeries...

PART I

The Castle Rockland – Isabella's Treasures – The Lock of Hair Gladiator and Black Medallion

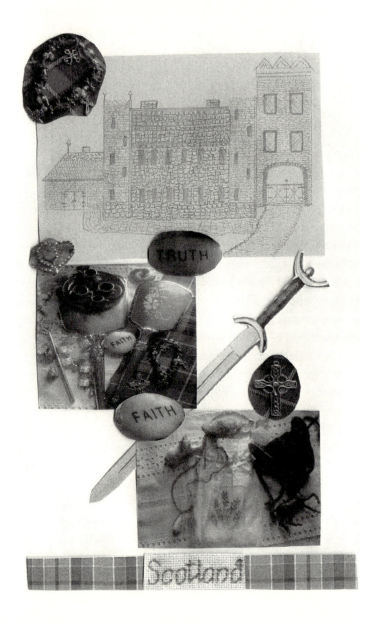

PART I

Isabella held the parchment paper in her hands opening and closing it, disbelieving what she had just read; it had been years since she had felt such gripping fear and *now* the fear was back - *in full force!*

The Queen summoned Rosetta to fetch William to meet her in the *main* library; it was urgent! The fire was crackling and the room was *warm*, but a *chill* had formed around Isabella's heart - she could no longer *hold back her tears.* As William rushed into the room; he took one look at Isabella and ran to her side!

"Isabella! Lass, what is wrong? What has happened?" he asked as he knelt down beside his Queen. Isabella was too distraught to speak; all she could do was hand him the *paper*! William's face fell as he read the news about the King; King Rennie had *died suddenly* - late into the night! William looked in disbelief staring down at the paper, it was *real* – the *seal* of the Queen of the Peoplefolk was on the parchment paper!

Suddenly William started pacing across the room in front of the large old stone fireplace. Nervously the dogs stirred by the fireplace looking up at him, watching him closely, *instinctively* sensing something - knowing *all is not right* with the Mistress and their Master! Stopping - William stretched his long muscular arms out leaning his hands against the rough stones of the fireplace; making sure to keep his back to Isabella, he closed his eyes in an effort to hide his own sorrow! He knew what this meant for Isabella - for now - there was no *consoling her*; no easing her pain!

The longtime friendship of the King of the Peoplefolk and Isabella's family had been a blessing for them; he was one of their *greatest allies*! The King had been a great man and a great *influence* in the lives of the Faeryfolk; this was indeed a day to mourn!

William went to Isabella holding her as she cried; the Queen cried for many things that morning - for herself, for Queen Ivy, Prince Davey and for her people!

"Isabella, my darling wife, I am so sorry – there are no words, there is no way of reckoning with this news at this *moment in* time!" said King William as he choked back tears of his own! The first hours of daylight were spent confined within the private chambers of the King and Queen; they were not only mourning a *great KING* but for a very *dear friend* whom they loved like one of *their own kind*!

It was spring and normally a time of joy and celebration for the Healing Faeries; a time for planting and sowing the seeds of their trade; remedies for *healing*! But William knew this would affect all their clan deeply when the news spread and William *also knew* Isabella had to go to the Queen and her son Prince Davey - right away!

William was right; it wasn't long before his Queen asked the head stableman to prepare her horse Gladiator for travel! Queen Isabella was 'gone like the wind' riding her horse across the rugged coastline heading straight towards the Castle Rockland with no time to spare! Immediately King William sent riders to follow Isabella at a distance - he was already *afraid* for his Queen; he knew her passion and he knew her *determination* and most of all - her *love* for her people!

By the time Isabella arrived at the gates her veiled hair had escaped out of its *braided twirl*; her long massive curls hung down to her waist and her hooded cloak - which was tied at the nape; *floated* in the wind behind her! Eyes glazed like a *wild woman* she certainly did not look like the Queen that she was; but Isabella did not care!

Immediately one of the guards recognized her as she passed through the gates and quickly took care of her horse while *another* escorted her inside. The servants were a little taken aback by the *sight* of her apparel but *discretely* ushered her quietly to the Queens personal chambers without a word!

Alone in the privacy of Queen Ivy's chamber the two women were able to share their true feelings – *mourning* the King *together*. Queen Ivy had told her the King had not been well and had taken to his bed; she had not called upon Isabella or the Healing Clan for she thought it was just a cold coming on – *a little congestion!* Her husband had said 'not to worry', that he was fine; but it *was not so*...The King had passed away through the night and Queen Ivy had never even got a chance to say *goodbye*! Isabella could sense her loss and feel her pain and was prepared to try everything she could to ease it!

When Isabella had left her home, the Castle Heatheren she had been in a hurry but had grabbed her most valued 'healing tools' in a leather pouch she always kept by her side...Along with her favorite *healing* stones Isabella had brought her favorite oil, the oil of *Frankincense*!

The *incense* and oil of Frankincense were very sacred to Isabella and very hard to acquire! *Together*, they were used to cleanse, purify, soothe and anoint areas in ones *heart* and *home* to make way for future blessings to be bestowed upon them...

The cold damp room was starting to warm up as Isabella added more wood on the fire; the warmth and the aroma of the oil mingled softly, hovering, gently nudging at *your soul*! The only other person in the room with them was the Queen's oldest, dearest housekeeper and loyal longtime servant – Jenny.

First Isabella placed the *Clear Quartz crystal* and the *Rose Quartz* in the Queens hands asking her to just hold them for *a while*. Then she brought out her special *Amethyst* necklace for the Queen to wear; the one Nanny Belle had given Isabella when she had returned home. Isabella also knew that Queen Ivy was open to the *healing* methods of Isabella and the Healing Faeries and therefore was able to have the *faery faith* and *trust* she needed to feel the benefits right away!

Next, Jenny and Isabella made some lemon tea with one of the herbs called Lemon Balm; it was a soothing mix, especially when blended with a *hint* of Lavender!

One would not think that tea had such 'healing properties' but when one drinks these *special blends* of herbal teas each blend can heal the person *inside* and *out* surrounding them with the soothing aroma; *filling* them with love, nourishment and protection, giving them that 'extra strength' they need in order to do the *healing*! It's the same with the 'crystals'; when one *opens their minds* to healing it's just a 'matter of time' before they can feel the difference as the *crystals* and the *teas* do their work!

Finally when Isabella saw that the Queen was sleeping *soundly* she told Jenny that she needed to go see Prince Davey; the Queens son! Knowing the Prince; Isabella thought for sure he would be having a sleepless night too... Isabella knew Queen Ivy would be fine in the loving and capable hands of the housekeeper but felt *she too* must be *silently grieving* for his Majesty and longtime friend; King Rennie! This was indeed a time for mourning and sadness!

Quietly Isabella left through the carved archway and out through the large doors that led out into the dimly lit corridor. It was now late into the night and she felt tired, sad and *lonesome* for William.

As Isabella turned the corner she was taken by surprise' to see a girl coming down the hall towards her! As the girl hurried passed her; a strange *feeling* came over the Queen. With Isabella's keen sense of 'second sight' as the Healing Faeries called it she felt something was not right! She quickly turned to watch the girl *servant* go down the hall.

She was not your typical servant; she was tall and beautiful with small dainty features like that of the Faeryfolk; *like that* of the *Healing Faeries*! The girl must have sensed something too for she turned around to stare at Isabella and then hurriedly disappeared down the stone stairway.

Isabella felt so troubled she felt compelled to go back to the Queen's chambers to talk with Jenny right away; so she backtracked along the elaborately decorated hallway not even taking in the beauty surrounding her!

Isabella was *visibly shaking* as her sinking foreboding thoughts mingled with the dampness of the old Castle! *Finally* she came to the large outer doors to the Queens chambers; trying not to disturb the sleeping Queen - she quietly motioned for Jenny to follow her out into the sitting room!

Trying to keep calm she asked Jenny anxiously, "Jenny, who is that tall pretty servant girl I just passed coming down hall? I don't recall seeing her before!" she added keenly watching the tired eyes of the old housekeeper.

Jenny nodded her head knowingly; slowly finding her voice, "Oh your Grace, that is the new girl, Lily; she is here to help me for I am getting too old and cannot do this work alone anymore!" Jenny said as she went on to explain more, "The Lass came looking for work a fortnight ago and Queen Ivy took *a liking* to the girl right away!" she answered in her strong Scottish accent. "The Queen said she reminded her - a 'wee bit' like you; she was strong, youthful and knew a bit of everything, *even* about the healing ways!" she added with certainty.

Isabella held her breath for a moment; then spoke, "Jenny did she *ever* help you with the needs of your Majesty the King and your Highness?" she asked *fear* rising within her.

"Yes, your Grace she was hired to do that very thing!" she answered slowly.

"Jenny!" Isabella said trying not to frighten her. "Did she ever give the King anything for his cold?" asked Isabella.

Jenny started to think - her blue eyes getting *wider* as she answered, "Aye, your Grace, she gave him some hot broth and some tea on the night he died! She wanted to help; she made it herself that night!" she added grasping her wrinkled hands to her shawl and holding it close. Isabella quickly saw the fear in the old woman's eyes and gently grasped her arms.

"Jenny we must not say a word to the Queen just yet! Do not let Lily back into this room do you hear? I shall return and knock *three* times so you shall know it's me!" Isabella said as she hurried out the door! She hesitated just long enough to hear Jenny adjust the lock behind her!

Isabella then tried to alert as many of the servants throughout the Castle as she could to help her find the raven-haired girl named Lily!

As Isabella entered the main hall of the grand entrance she ran into the head servant and *trustworthy friend* of the King coming through the large main doors of the Castle! Running towards him; trying not to startle him Isabella urgently asked him about the girl, "Oh James, dear James; I need to find the new servant girl Lily, have you seen her?"

"Yes, my Lady, an odd thing has just happened...she has left our service!" he exclaimed mystified.

"James, she was just upstairs less than an hour ago – are you sure?" asked Isabella *surprised* by his answer.

"Yes, my Lady, I sent McCabe my night watchman to fetch her horse – she said her Mother was sick and she felt she had to leave right away and to tell the Queen; she was sorry!" he added.

"Thank you James!" said Isabella in a hoarse voice just above a whisper. Ghostlike Isabella brushed past James and stepped out into the Castle courtyard; it was almost sunrise and she was so tired, so confused, but she had to *stay alert* to think of what she should do next!

She couldn't prove anything and may just be over-exaggerating *her thoughts* but, "Could this girl have poisoned the King?"

Isabella would have to be sure of her feelings to make that statement' to the Queen. For now, she must go tell Jenny what she has found!

Jenny being the loyal and faithful servant as she was - fully understood, telling Isabella not to worry; they would guard their *secret thoughts* for now - the girl was gone and that was one good thing! Isabella then gathered her plaid cloak around her and slipped her leather pouch over her shoulder; she desperately needed to go find the Prince; *now!*

The old housekeeper told Isabella she would find him in the stables at this hour of the morning and she wasn't surprised. He loved his horses like Isabella and he liked being near them and going for early morning rides. His favorite horse was a stallion *like no other.* The horse was a beautiful breed; his *long wild mane* hung half way down his massive back; his brilliant color of blue-black bringing him his *noble name* of Black Medallion.

As Isabella was weaving her way around the Castle grounds Isabella's thoughts went back to the day when her Mother had given her a *braided lock* of hair from her 'favorite Stallion's mane' on Prince Edward Island and the day that Prince Davey had wanted a 'lock of her hair' before she left Scotland! It was a 'symbol' for them both and one they *both believed in.*

For the Healing Faeries it was a 'symbol' they left to let one know *you would see them again*; but for *centuries* within the royal families *noble* men *and* women believed that 'strength and courage' could be passed on through the *gift* of *one's hair*; also the fact that one's hair is *eternal* – <u>it never dies</u>!

As Isabella entered the stables the *smell* of the horses, a familiar smell she loved *soothed* her dampened spirits. Just inside Cullen the head stableman stood grooming the horses. He turned as he heard someone approaching.

"Ah, my Queen good morn' to you!" said Cullen as he greeted Isabella with a bow. "Tis' always a pleasure to see you my Lass!" he added. In return Isabella gave him a hug; she had known him for such a long time, he was indeed a true friend!

"Good morn' to you Cullen!" Isabella said as she mustered up a smile for him. "I am looking for Prince Davey this morn', have you seen him?" she asked.

"Aye, the Prince is in the back riding stables getting ready for his morning ride!" he answered.

Isabella looked up at Cullen sadly and with tears forming in her eyes, no longer able to stop herself, she said, "What is to become of us all Cullen; *without* the King? Will Prince Ivan come home from France? Will it ever be the same ever again?" Not waiting for an answer Isabella continued, "Today is what the Faeries call 'a new beginning' – with each *new sunrise* we can begin again! But can we Cullen, can we?" cried Isabella unashamed as she broke down in tears in front of this big rugged man.

"Aye Lass, we can, we can!" answered Cullen as he reached out for her. "You know you just have to *believe it*! You know nothing happens without a reason – *all is for not*, if life were to stay the same my Queen it would ruin us! Take this day as a new day like the Healing Faeries have been tellin' us and find 'life' in it!" he added strongly; dropping his grasp on her arms, he swiftly turned back to his grooming...

Isabella stood there for a few seconds longer staring at Cullen's strong back and thought about his name and its *meaning*; it was derived from the ole' Scottish meaning – 'a young, handsome animal/beast'... He must have been *very* handsome as a young man and now with his age and wisdom he was indeed a *noble man* to look up to!

Isabella did not keep him talking for she had seen his own tears starting to form in the corners of his wrinkled blue eyes! He was right; she had to keep the 'faery faith' as he said - she must remain strong, true and *believe* that this all had *a purpose* to it!

Isabella left then and continued on to the back of the stables where the riding horses were kept; it was time to find the Prince and *time* for her to console *him*!

Prince Davey was a *true faery faith friend* and as a *true Patriot Queen* of the Healing Faeries she must 'pull herself together'! Stricken with the grief of the sudden death of his *Father* - Isabella knew that their days of *idleness* and *playfulness* that they had both known; were gone! Now was the time to be women and men; the time to let the *warrior inside – come out*! Like the 'hair that endures' – they too had to go on! Now they had to be the *strong courageous ones* like their Fathers, Mothers and Grandparents *before them*!

For a fleeting moment Isabella's thoughts went back to the days when they had played in the Castle together, when they were young! She remembered the day that he had told her that 'her hair' was as *wild and unruly* as his stallions' and that her *spirit* was the same and he *hoped - she would never change*! He had even tried to *kiss* her that day - but Isabella had run from him laughing saying he would turn into a *Faerie child* if he kissed her! Instead she had given him a 'lock of her hair' to keep; for even in their youth and *innocent hearts* both Isabella and the Prince fully understood the meaning! It was hard to believe it had been *seven years ago*! They had both grown up a lot since then and especially in the last two years since Isabella had came back to Scotland and became *Queen*!

To Isabella, Prince Davey was a gem! He had been a *charming boy* and had turned into a *charming young man*. Everyone liked him and Isabella was blessed to have him as a friend!

Queen Isabella walked up to him in the barn; bidding a 'good day' to his stablemen! They immediately bowed down before her as Isabella, gathering her skirts about her; *smiled* and they in turn smiled back *politely* making haste to return to their busy morning chores! The Prince stopped what he was doing and gallantly kissed Isabella's hand - also *bowing* before her.

She then hugged him to her and told him how sorry she was about his Father, "Oh Davey...I am so *sorry!*" she said as she buried her head in his shoulder. And as if on cue she then reached inside her cloak pocket and out came a lock of *his hair* he had given her so long ago! It was wrapped in a piece of his family Clan tartan; the plaid a bit *tattered* and *faded.*

"Oh Isabella, you never seize to amaze me! How do you always know what is needed?" he asked smiling and although he was being charming, she saw the telltale signs of *red* around his eyes.

"I have brought something else with me that tis' even more meaningful!" she said softly. She dug once again deep within her pocket and took out a small pouch. Isabella handed him the leather pouch. He reached inside and found a *ring;* it was gold with a large *diamond* in the middle...He looked up at Isabella with a puzzled look on his face.

Isabella asked if they could walk together and find a place where they may sit and talk; so Prince Davey took her to the orchards nearby where there were lovely wooden benches to rest on. The grass was wet from the early morning rain but the sun's heat had dried the benches and the warm sweet *smell* of the *rain* still lingered in the air!

Once seated, Isabella started to explain, *"This ring was given to me by your Father, King Rennie when I first came to visit you two years ago! Do you remember my first visit after I arrived back from Prince Edward Island?"* she asked.

"Yes, I *remember.*" he said.

"Well your Father gave me this ring and told me that I was to be the 'keeper of it' till the day he was no longer with us!" Isabella said with astonishment still in her voice. "I was puzzled and asked him why and *why me*? And *what* was *I* supposed *to do with it*?" continued Isabella.

"What did Father say Issy?" he asked.

"Well he told me it had been *his* Fathers and I was to pass it on to one of his sons' – the *one* who would be left standing by his Mother's side, the one whose heart was *not* ruled by *material things*!" she answered sullenly.

"Well Isabella, my Brother is on his way *as we speak*!" he added.

"Aye, I know Davey, I know!" she said. "But *I already know* who has to have this ring!" As Isabella passed it into his hand she added, "You do not have to wear it *now*, but take it, *please*!" Isabella urged.

"Okay, I will take it Isabella, for you know I trust you *like no other*!" he added with a more serious look in his eyes!

"There is something else I have to share with you! I am not sure how to tell you..." as Isabella gathered her courage, "I have this feeling about one of the servants...and about your *Fathers' death*!"

"Isabella, what are you talking about?" the Prince asked; *concern* rising in his voice.

"There was a new girl servant named Lily that looked after your Father the night he died; she had made him *tea and broth*...and *already* she has fled the Castle with an excuse of her failing Mother's health! She left truly in the middle of the night - last night; by horse!" Isabella stated as she tried to catch her breath. "Thus far I have only talked to Jenny about it and *now you!*" she added.

The Prince stared at her in shock *disbelieving* the meaning! "Aye, I have seen her – the new servant, the *pretty one* - yes she was hired to help Jenny – I...I think I am going to *be ill!*" he added. "Oh, Isabella, Mother will never live to hear this news...she is so distraught – we must *not* tell her! It will push her over the edge!" he said as his face suddenly turned ashen.

"I had a feeling in the hall when I saw her...and when I put an alert out in the Castle to find her...I did not tell anyone the reason! Then when I found James he told me about her *quick* departure!" Isabella explained as she pulled her shawl tightly around her.

"Oh Isabella, *please* do not say another word out loud – *for now*! She has fled – good riddance! Until we have my Brother here let us keep it to ourselves!" the Prince added.

"I should not have mentioned my fears; I am truly sorry Davey!" Issy said hastily. "I cannot stand the thought *if this is true* – the meaning for us all!" she said with a flat tone. She then grabbed her dear friend to her holding him as they shared their grief once more - *vowing* not to mention another word for fear the *truth* be known and the sheer ugliness of it all!

For now, they *all* had to wait! They had summoned his older brother from France to come home to Scotland *as soon as possible*! The Prince was on his way and would arrive by sail on the ship called the *Alabaster*; which was known for its great *speed*.

That week *everything* had come to a standstill in the Castle. Isabella had sent word to William that she was staying on for a few more days to help out and to her surprise the *very next day* a carriage was sent with some of Isabella's things along with a message from William in his *own handwriting*!

"My Dearest Isabella, *please forgive me* for I am not as good with pen in hand' or verse like you!" he stated. Isabella smiled to herself as she read on...

Remember to wear your Jade, I put it in your bag
It's the stone of *Healing Hearts* and *Mending Souls*
It's the one that wears like Gold
The one to wear closest to your heart...
The Amethyst stone to help you sleep
The Amber to keep you strong and safe
These will guide you for tonight
For I will be there by day's end; on Morrows' night!

Love, Your William, Your King...

"Oh, my darling..." he added, "Inside your pouch and bag of silk you will find more of your *herbs and teas*, I hope you like your other *surprises* too! I have sent your blue tea set; mirror and brush set, your favorite *sun hat* for your garden walks and the 'little things' you love!"

Isabella held the note as she looked down at the Prince Edward Island tartan scarf he had sent; she had left so fast she had forgotten to wear it! She silently thanked him - as usual he knew what she needed the most and *when*! He had also sent a pouch of her *favorite jewelry*! Isabella was known for wearing so much jewelry she looked more like a 'gypsy' than a *Queen,* but - that was our Isabella! She was different; she wore her *true colors* on her sleeve and was not liken to any other Queens; in <u>*any Realm*</u>. There was something about Isabella that made her stand out and people tended to listen to her and follow her long before she sat on the throne. She had a way with the Peoplefolk *and* Faeryfolk alike. There was this charm about her that drew people to her. William himself had felt it the *first day* he met her!

William had also sent some special 'wine'; made with a special *secret* blend of ingredients which was *created* by the Healing Faeries! If you had ever had the *chance* to 'partake' – they said you would want 'more and more' and it was widely known throughout the Kingdom as *exquisite!* William had slyly added this 'gift' for Isabella and the Queen; it was filled with all sorts of *healing properties* which *aids* in the healing process, as Isabella was 'wittingly known to quote'!

The Queen felt so loved and blessed as she reread William's note! Isabella was happy also to see he had sent her *dear friend* and personal servant *Rosetta* to help her out! She had been with her since the day Isabella had become *Queen;* choosing *not to* return to France with the others!

Over the next few days Isabella made her presence known in the Castle. She got things in order *quickly* for the servants respected her and they knew how much the King had *valued* their relationship. Prince Davey and Queen Ivy were glad to have her there and when King William and Nanny Belle arrived; together they started preparing for the vast burial ceremony and the arrival of Prince Ivan from France!

Everyone expected the eldest son to become the next *King* and everyone was *thankful* he was coming! The Queen had never thought she would be *left alone* – the King had been her rock and he had ran things with such *master and ease* she wondered how anyone could replace him!

Finally, the Prince arrived along with Emilie! He told them Gabriel and Cecile would be travelling through the *Faery Realm* and were expected later that day! By this time inside the Castle was filling up with guests and the area surrounding the Castle was dotted with caravans and tents as the Kings' followers came to bid their *last* farewell!

This normally would have been such a joyous occasion for everyone to be together once again and friends and family relished their time the best they could; under the circumstances. The gentlemen spent the first night locked up in the drawing room by the fire with their spirits' in hand till the *wee hours* of the morning!

The ladies spent most of *their time* in the Queens private quarters *sewing* and talking with her and of course with Queen Isabella; who not only shared her Healing Faery energies and remedies with them but also her *special* 'Healing Wine'- of which *they all partook*!

Emilie and Cecile had brought *gifts* from France for all of them! Of course *more French Lavender*; some new warm clothes and woolens for the coming *nippy* winter, French lace, scarves and some of their *best* French wines!

Emilie had brought Isabella a *special* gift of a 'small purse' with embroidered beads on it in the form of a *star shaped* flower! She knew how much Isabella liked small fine things! They even had some *Gold* from Spain; along with special jewelry items handpicked in *both Silver and Gold*! Isabella loved *Silver* and Queen Ivy loved the *Gold*!

Emilie was also glad to see Isabella was still wearing her *Amber ring* she had given her before she had left France. She also secretly loved the thought of 'being back' on her Scottish soil and had not realized how much she had missed her homeland and the *company* of the other women she had come to *love*! Cecil fit right in with everyone and of course once she started playing her *harp* for them; everyone loved her *even more*. She was very gifted and talented but shy about her *extraordinary* French *natural beauty*. Isabella could see why Gabriel had fallen *in love with her*!

The Queen was as happy as she *could* be to be with her closest and dearest friends; the tragedy bringing her two sons' together along with her only other close family members; her sister Ronalda and her sister-in-law Doreen.

That next day everyone busily prepared themselves for the burial ceremonies; each in *their own way*. Prince Davey was still out riding his black Stallion and was waiting until the very last minute to get ready! Queen Ivy had been up through the night and had gotten ready early. She had strict instructions for all her servants on how she wanted things carried out 'to the letter' for her late husband, King Rennie's funeral! Emilie and Prince Ivan had also had an early start and were the first ones down to the dining hall for breakfast along with Gabriel and Cecile!

William and Isabella lingered in the privacy of their quarters in the southern wing of the Castle. They briefly wanted to share their *experiences* of the night before; before going down for breakfast.

"William how did you make out with your *group of men* in the Library last night?" asked Isabella as she tried to sit still long enough for Rosetta to attend to her - *unruly* hair!

"It was so great to see everyone under the *circumstances* Issy!" he said sleepily. "It *was* a late night – I apologize for that my sweet!" he added.

"How was the conversation? How were Gabriel and Prince Ivan doing?" she asked.

"You are certainly full of *questions* this morning Lass!" he laughed.

"Well I am sure they shared a lot *considering* how late you were!" she teased back.

"Well to tell you the truth it was a little strange towards the end of our night!" he answered. "At first everyone was filling in the news about how everyone was and then it *strangely* turned when the Queen's brother-in-law, Duncan's conversation *turned angry* towards the brothers!" he added. "Duncan was very much interested in what was going to happen to he and his wife's *monies* very specifically once Prince Ivan became King!" he stated feeling the embarrassment of it once again.

"Really, Willy..." Isabella answered; not really asking a question but more of a statement. "I also found Doreen very much pushing Queen Ivy last night to talk about what will happen next while the other Ladies and I kept trying to keep the conversation 'light and airy' for Queen Ivy; to keep her mind off, today!" she added. "You could tell Doreen was certainly not interested in our *banter* and our *secret pleasure* to be with one another even under these circumstances!" Isabella said reassuringly. "I truly liked the Queens sister Ronalda; she was so witty' and made us laugh which we all needed! And I want to thank you again for thinking to send our Healing Faery wine William – everyone *enjoyed* it!" Isabella added with a *gleam* in her eye! "I'm sorry my sweet I am talking to much as usual; pray do tell me more!" she said looking up at him with a loving glance; through the mirror!

"Well," said King William, "After the conversation began the night pretty well went from *bad to worse* as King Ivan abruptly got up and excused himself, bid us goodnight and left us there; our mouths *gaping!*" he said as he finished putting on his overcoat. "Very strange indeed!" he added as he left the room.

Isabella reached up and touched Rosetta's hand and stopped her from continuing on her hair.

"What is it *your Highness*?" she asked.

"Rosetta I know you are a loyal friend and servant of mine but I know you must hear things *in the Castle...*" she said slowly. "Have you heard anything about the unrest or feelings being shared among the Castle Rockland's household servants?" asked Isabella.

"Only that they are very much afraid for their own wellbeing and of course wonder how it will be under *new rule!*" she added. "They all know Prince Davey and feel comfortable with him and are *unsure* of Prince Ivan!" Rosetta said *too quickly*! Rosetta busied herself as she continued helping Queen Isabella dress for the ceremony and kept the rest of her thoughts *to herself*!

Rosetta was glad to see everyone *as well* and in this household and in Isabella's Castle Heatheren; as always the 'closely knit' servants *mingled* with the royalty! Their *outstanding loyalty* 'knew no bounds' – their love and their devotion for those who kept them in their service was outstanding; *especially* in times of need!

But between Rosetta and those around her no one was *more shocked* than Isabella for what happened *just days* following the Kings burial!

The ceremony had been very beautiful and *typical* on such a grand scale fit for the royalty and sovereignty of a *departed King*! The Royal court; the dress, the extravagance and the twelve Scottish Pipers, at his side! It was an amazing ritual to be a witness to. The mass of people surrounding the burial grounds was truly amazing and the guards had to stay on top of the crowds to let those closest to the King pass by.

Everyone who was there had expected Prince Ivan to become the *next King* for he was the oldest and the next in line; but the shock was - *he did not want to be King* and he planned on returning to France; as soon as possible! That left the youngest son, Prince Davey in line. Isabella was the first to hear it from the Queen herself.

The Queen stood by her bed in her chambers. She looked over at Isabella and solemnly stated, "Isabella I summoned you for I have no once else to confide in – I am very distraught about my Son's decision! I know you cannot *force* someone to become King if they do not want to or to *follow* in their Father's footsteps! I do not know how I am going to handle this..." the Queen added as she tried to compose herself; visibly shaken, by the *latest tale of events*.

Isabella stood quietly as she struggled to find the right words to console the Queen. She had already heard through Rosetta that Prince Ivan, Emilie, Gabriel and Cecile had left that very morning! They had gone to see Queen Ivy but did not wake Isabella to say goodbye; which was a *shock for her already*!

Finally Isabella summoned the courage to ask, "What does Prince Davey say? How does he feel about being the next in line?"

"Well," Queen Ivy answered slowly, "He says he is *ready* and that he can *do the job*! He has watched his Father and he has always shown 'more interest' in our lands and the Kingdom than his Brother!" she added.

"*Aye*, would you like me to speak with him?" asked Isabella.

"Oh yes, would you go to him?" she pleaded.

"Aye, Your Majesty I will go right away!" Isabella answered; knowing the trust she had just given her and knowing that her loyal youngest Son must *need someone to talk* to at this time!

Isabella found him out in the garden. He had a grin on his face when he saw her...he was always glad to see her. He was always so *positive* and *good* when things got rough! Queen Isabella *hugged him.*

"Can we talk?" she asked him.

"Of course, Isabella!" he answered; taking her arm he led her to some wooden seats; by the pond.

"How do you *really* feel about becoming King?" asked Isabella; as she sat down beside him.

He had the same humor as Isabella and tried to make light of it, "Oh I know I can do it; not as good as *my Father* but a *lot better* than my Brother *ever could!*" he stated flatly with a grin.

"I'm the Prince left *wearing the ring!*" he added, holding up his hand to show her.

Isabella smiled looking at his hand and said, "Oh Davey I know you can do it - you will make a *great King!* You have stood by your Mother and Father all this time and I know you have partaken in many wise decisions regarding the Kingdom and your people!"

Together, Isabella and the Prince went to see the Queen; their plans had to happen quickly, leaving the *throne empty* for any length of time was *not good*! And knowing the shrouded mystery surrounding the King's death – Isabella and Prince Davey *felt the urgency*!

When they arrived at his Mother's chambers they were surprised to find his Aunt Doreen and her husband, Duncan coming out from his Mother's quarters. He knew they had been *fairly* close but was surprised to see them still there when all the others had *returned* to their homes following the burial.

The Queen was sitting near the window staring out into the cool damp morning; it was raining and you could tell she had been *crying*.

"Mother, are you alright?" Prince Davey asked as he quickly brought a warm woolen shawl to put around her shoulders.

"Aye Laddie I am fine! I am fine..." she added *not convincingly*.

"We just saw Aunt Doreen leaving, are things alright between *you all* Mother?" he asked.

"Oh, just the normal!" said the Queen! "She is always concerned with my health and well being and my plans; especially *now* your Father has gone!" she added solemnly.

"What do you mean, Mother?" asked Prince Davey.

"Well she was *always* concerned of *monetary values* and how much money and lands we had and about 'material things'... But now she is concerned with what will happen to her now that *her Brother* is no longer *King*? She wanted to know if they will still be 'taken care of' since she was the *Sister* of the King! I assured her things would go on as they had but I kept feeling she was searching for something *more* from me Davey!" she answered with a puzzled look on her face. "She was most disappointed in your Brother not taking over the throne and went on about it for some time! Even going so far as to say your Brother knew how to handle his monies and his properties - *unlike* you!"

"That *is strange* Mother! I am sorry you had to hear all that so soon since Father has only been gone from us for such a short time!" Prince Davey answered; his mind also scrambling to figure it out for her.

Isabella also listened intently to the conversation; a feeling of foreboding *enveloping* her soul, like a *'Faery knowing'* that something was not *quite right*!

Isabella wanted to change the 'energy' of the room for the Queen and her Son so she suggested they have some *herbal tea* brought up to them! While they summoned Jenny; getting young Rosetta to help her - the Prince himself added more wood on the fire in the old stone fireplace while Isabella lit some comfy candles about the room and burnt some *incense oil*! They all needed some relaxing quiet time – some time to *reflect* on all they had just gone through!

Sadly, Isabella and William had to leave the Castle Rockland the following day; they had plenty of catching up to do, with their own duties as *King and Queen*!

The following week there was to be a *ceremony*; a swearing in of the throne and the *crowning of a*

36

King! The news *spread* but so did the *uneasiness* surrounding the Kingdom of Scotland! They all knew things would change in the Kingdom; but no one knew things would change *so quickly*!

PART II

Gabriel – Queen Isabella – King William

PART II

It was only three days after Isabella and William had returned to the Castle Heatheren that William had a surprise visit from his *trusty friend* Roland - who had just arrived *back* from France. Roland had heard a *rumor* while there from one of Prince Ivan's men about an unrest that had started *months* before King Rennie had died; but *now* there was a *plot* to destroy the Kingdom of the Healing Faeries and a plan to take back the *land all along the coast of Scotland*! The young King *acted fast*!

First of all, William gathered some of his finest men from their Faery Realm and left right away heading for Prince Davey and Queen Ivy's Castle! *But on the way* they met Prince Davey and a band of his men 'fleeing for their lives' heading towards *their* Castle! There had been a *raid* in the middle of the night and the Prince had narrowly escaped with some of his men! Luckily his *Mother*, the Queen of the Peoplefolk had been *away* visiting *her Sisters' home* in the town nearby! Already, they had sent some riders to escort Queen Ivy to the coast to board the next ship; heading for France, with 'little *nothing*' but a trunk of her clothing that she had taken with her!

William and Isabella had to think fast! Prince Davey had narrowly escaped the 'band of Peoplefolk' called the *Mandolins!* Just hearing the name '*Mandolins*' made Isabella's hair *stand up* on the back of her neck! She had never known the 'name' of the men who had overthrown their lands and her Clan till William told her *years later*! Now she knew it was time to *prepare* for the *worst*! They had to prepare for the fight *of their lives...*

That night Prince Davey; his personal guards, William, Roland, Isabella and Nanny Belle met alone first to discuss what happens next in this *untimely* upheaval! Prince Davey had not even had time to be *crowned* KING! It was a grave matter for his household and the Kingdom of the Peoplefolk to be left unattended and the *throne empty*!

King William sat at the head of the long wooden table trying to form his thoughts; knowing this was *just the beginning* of *a long fight* for them!

He started the meeting in his strong even Scottish voice, "Ye all cannot know how sorry I am to see us meeting *once again* under these circumstances! First of all I am so *grateful* and *thankful* that Prince Davey is here with us tonight and Queen Ivy is *safe!*" he said as he solemnly looked at each one of them; his eyes coming to rest on the Prince, sitting beside him...

"Hear! Hear!" each murmured *softly* - agreeing with William.

King William continued, "I also want to commend him on his *bravery a*s he went ahead *on his own stance* and heeded the *words* of *his Father;* as you have already heard!" the King added.

King Rennie had taught his son well and *luckily* the Prince had listened and before his Father was *even buried;* he had hidden most of the Kings *wealth* and his most *precious possessions* as instructed! "It is such loyalty like this that knows *no bounds;* to listen and follow orders, not knowing *WHY!* But, Prince Davey *did just that* and that is the kind of leadership we need in our fight for *FREEDOM!*" King William added; his heart filling up with *pride.*

As Isabella listened her mind went racing back to the day King Rennie's own Sister had asked the Queen openly what was to 'become of her monies' now that her *Brother was dead*! He had always allotted monies, properties and protection *for her* and *her family*... "Why had the King asked his Son to *bury his riches*? Did he know that *someone* was trying to *kill* him?" Isabella asked herself; her thoughts racing inside, for answers! The *plot* was dangerously thickening and now it was time for Prince Davey and Isabella to share their *thoughts* with the others; the *possibility* that King Rennie *had been murdered*! She could no longer hold back her *tongue*!

"William, my King, may I beg to interrupt with *a subject* far more *graver* and more *shocking* which has been held back till this moment!" hurried Isabella not sure if she had left these *hidden thoughts*; too late.

She looked to the Prince for some support as she cautiously went on... "I am praying I have not left this *too late*..." she added, "On the night I arrived at Queen Ivy's Castle I saw a *new servant girl* whom I did not recognize and I felt 'ill at ease' about her!

With my *Faery Knowing* – my *'gift'* of *second sight* I inquired about her and James said she had fled in the *late of night'* not long after I had saw her! The girl told him she had to *take leave* to go care for her sick Mother!" said Isabella as she glanced around the room watching them all intently. *"Then to find* – she had made a *special* broth of soup and tea for King Rennie the *very night* he died!" she uttered as her voice continued, gaining momentum, "I *BELIEVE;* the King was MURDERED!" she added finishing up with the most *unspeakable* words, imaginable!

There was not a sound in the room as Prince Davey jumped in for her, "It t'was I who told Queen Isabella *not to say a word'* till we sort things out; before uttering *such a theory* – and now perhaps it was not in good judgment since I could have tried to piece the puzzle *together* after Isabella told me; hence my Father asking me to bury our treasures!" he said in such a *sorrowful voice.*

Everyone's face was in *shock* as King William spoke, "Nay, we cannot go back; we must only go forward with this grave matter! It still does not tell us the 'whole story' but it is indeed such *shocking news* as to make me want to stop and take some time for *all of us* - a chance *for us; to gather ourselves!*" he said as his voice fell to a *stammering* low murmur.

Then taking control again he said, "Isabella, fetch Rosetta to bring us tea, some left over's *and spirits'* - it is much needed at this time!" Not a muscle flinched in William's face as he kept his head held high and his eyes staring *straight* at Isabella!

As Queen Isabella left the room he turned to the Prince and Nanny Belle... "I am indeed thankful Queen Ivy is not present at our table tonight; however Prince Davey I am *truly sorry* for this *discovery* and how you have had to keep this hidden *inside you!*" replied the King.

Nanny Belle was the next one to speak, "William, it must have been *hard* for Isabella to keep such thoughts inside *herself also* and now that it is out we have got to take *immediate action* and heed the *call* of the Healing Faeries; throughout the Kingdom!" she added forcefully. "I am *so sorry* Prince Davey to hear these words!" she added in a graver tone. She went to him and *hugged him to her*!

"Aye, we have to join together - *more than ever now...*" said the Prince in a *hoarse voice.*

"We shall stand by your side *till the end*; you have done so much for our people!" King William answered. "Isabella and I have discussed it *many times* what we would do if anything were to ever happen again and *Mother* you and I know it is has been Isabella's destiny; to lead us to *FREEDOM!*" he added kno*wingly.* "We have always known *one way or another* deep in *our hearts'* it could one day come to this! When Isabella comes back – we will let her *lead us* with her great knowledge and her wisdom she has *inherited!*" he added humbly!

"So be it then! *So be it!*" Nanny Belle said to her Son.

The others in the room gathered together in *little groups* sharing their thoughts and taking in the *shock* of the latest news and *turn of events*! The Prince sat by himself in *silence* as he waited for the spirits' and refreshments to come; turning his Father's ring *over* and *over* on his left finger!

Suddenly an overwhelming feeling came over the Prince; not *sadness* but a feeling of 'POWER and HOPE' of which he was *surprised*; like 'a *Faery knowing*' or an *insight* that somehow; it was all <u>*meant to be*</u>! He also felt a greater *understanding* of the *teachings* of the Healing Faeries even though he had lived side by side with them for so long! Suddenly he felt a great feeling of *love, respect* and *gratitude* towards *Queen Isabella's Clan!*

Isabella came back with the refreshments and shared 'some of' *her plans* with them but felt she *could not* tell them *everything*! She wanted to protect them as long as she could! They would know soon enough the extent of this *CRY FOR FREEDOM* and how the outcome *would change each of their lives <u>forever</u>*!

Isabella was so thankful she had gone ahead and added more new chapters to their Healing Clan book! It now had some *new rules* and the latest 'creed' of the *Healing Faeries*! She was also thankful for all the *sound advice* from her Father and *the late* King Rennie! He had been a very smart man and it was because of him Isabella knew how to turn back *the pages of time*! It was time to do something *NO ONE* had *ever* done before in her Healing Clan *history* and something that would *NEVER* be done again!

Isabella talked to her closest confidents; King William, Nanny Belle, Prince Davey and all those she could trust to spread the word and make sure all her people obeyed the *rules of the land*! Now it was time for Queen Isabella to *RULE LIKE THE WIND* and to show *her Clan* how to do the same!

All their subjects were summoned to come to the *Castle Heatheren*! It was a *call* of the *Healing Faeries* like no other across the land of *time*! Although what they were about to do had never been done on such a 'grand scale' - the Clansmen and Clanswomen were *ready* and willing to fight for their *FREEDOM* and their land once again!

Freedom was the *symbol* for the Healing Faeries and they had to keep what they already had! Queen Isabella believed; '<u>*No matter how far, no matter how long it took, no matter 'what she had to do'; she would never give up on her dream*</u>!' THE DREAM; to *free her people <u>forever</u>*!

Immediately they all banned together knowing the first thing they had to do was 'set a trap'! They also had to hide all their *valuables*. Unlike the King and Queen of the Peoplefolk the Healing Faeries did not have as many 'riches' of material value but they had plenty of 'gifts' people had given to them along the way; more of the *homemade* value - unique, thoughtful, loving, healing momentums; for *memory's sake*!

On the whole their Castle was quite ordinary, 'down to earth' dotted with rustic strong homemade wooden furniture made from willow, ash and elder! Adorning the Castle was plenty of comfortable homemade pillows; blankets, handmade pottery throughout, lots of wood and rustic iron decorations, unique candelabras; even down to the smallest *details* and simple items like hinges were all *designed* and created by *their people*.

The Healing Faeries did value their 'way of life' so they hid all they could from view; things were stored in unlikely 'Faery hiding places' - around the *countryside*!

They worked long into that first night clearing all *the herbs* and *healing remedies*, preparing them for storage; trying to save them. All their food and winter supplies were moved to other *Havens* and 'wee Castle' *hiding places.*

Now they were ready for the *next plan*! First they sent their best riders and best warriors from both Prince Davey's *army* and King William's finest men to his Castle to try and talk with the head leader of the *Mandolins* and try to see what they could do to stop the upheaval - *before it got worse.*

The Queen of the Peoplefolk had lots of land and lots of riches to *negotiate* with and Prince Davey was prepared to reason with them if he could!

The Mandolins quickly sent their men *back with a message*; they only wanted to speak with *Prince Davey* since he was *supposed* to be the *upcoming KING*!

It was a dangerous thing to do but the Prince said he would go – he wanted to go and he would do it for his *Father*!

Before he left; King William and the Prince decided that the Healing Faery warriors would follow close behind his own army and be *ready* to back them up in case anything went wrong!

When Prince Davey arrived with his men everything looked *quiet!* As they *continued* coming to a halt just outside a clearing on the vast outer edge of the Castle walls; they waited for a signal, from within! But before they knew what had happened; they were *ambushed* from *all sides* and within minutes, *several men* were killed!

With the *onrush of fighting* the men regained their strength; anger edging them on; quickly retaliating, they sent the band of Mandolin's *retreating* - heading back to the safety of the Castle Rockland's walls! It all had happened *so fast* and when William's warriors arrived on the frontlines they had already heard the news that *the Prince* had been taken *prisoner* in his own Castle! It *was* as they had suspected; it had just been a ruthless *ploy* to *capture* Prince Davey!

Williams's friend Roland signaled to his Clansmen and the other *army of men* that were left; to *follow him*! They quickly took cover behind a mountain of craggy rocks strewn along the barren land by the Castle Rockland! Once they collected themselves they headed straight for their camp not far from the Castle; *hidden* in the glens.

When they arrived King William *knew* right away it was not good news! The news was not only *devastating* but now they knew they were in a *full scale war*! They quickly doused out all their campfires and reunited on the frontlines to discuss the next move.

Word *spread quickly*! It was time to put <u>into *motion*</u> the *plan* of the Healing Clan – time to *heed* the call; *the Freedom Cry* of the Healing Faeries!

The Mandolins did not know the FULL extent of the *creed* of the Secret of the Healing Faeries and their extraordinary powers' and had *never before witnessed* to this great length the 'Cry of Freedom'; or <u>the *force* behind it</u>! This was one of the greatest gifts' they had; their ability to become *invisible*! They would take them by *surprise* and *by force* but a *different* force; like the unforeseen force of *nature*; just like that of the *WIND*!

As they rode forward you could feel the *earth shake* – the winds were *blowing fiercely* and the tartans of the Healing Clan; draped across their chests, billowed out *proudly* behind them! They were *ready* to head the *call* of the Healing Faeries and *fight for their FREEDOM*! And now they must also avenge the death' of Prince Davies men and fight for Prince Davies *LIFE*!

This time the Mandolins were *not prepared* – for this battle was 'like no other'! The Healing Faeries were prepared to *use* everything that they could 'think of'; *to defend their right* to live in peace *and* harmony among the Peoplefolk.

The Healing Faeries left their horses hidden 'out of site' and *slowly*, <u>invisibly,</u> *stormed* the Castle! The Mandolins' were tough and rough men used to using brute force for everything...but they were *not* PREPARED for this *type* of invasion!

The first wave of the Healing Faery warriors got into the Castle <u>*using their invisible Healing Faery powers;*</u> among them was King William himself; with a team of *his closest men!*

Quickly, *invisibly* - they drugged the Mandolin's tea, food and *drinks* with herbal remedies to make the Band members *sleep!* Within minutes the only thing you could hear was the barking of the dogs within the Castle; the banter and the noisy feasting of Antoine's men; *silenced*! Their timing was perfect for the Mandolins were celebrating *their victory*!

While they *slept* they stole their food; their drinks, their weapons and *their horses*! Then using a special band of Healing Faery warriors set about to 'quickly' take as *many valuables* that were left out of the Castle Rockland; while they *had the time*!

It was an incredible *first siege* and at such a tremendous speed King William was very proud of every one of his men and *women* warriors! When the Mandolin's started to wake, the Castle was in a state of *mass confusion*! When the leader of the Mandolins' was found he immediately told his men to get a *message* to King Williams' Clansmen; that if this *form of siege* continued - they would *punish* Prince Davey!

But the Mandolins were no match 'in this state' with the *extraordinary powers* of the Healing Faeries! Not only did *their leader* Antoine find out about their missing food, horses and weapons; he quickly found out that Prince Davey had also *escaped* 'into the night air' *with* King William's men!

Immediately; the next day Antoine, the captain of the Mandolin's gathered his men; searched for more horses and then *joined forces* heading to the Castle Heatheren in *full speed*! He was angry and did not like to be made a fool of! He would show them he would *not stop* until he got what he wanted!

But to their *surprise* when they got there - <u>it was empty</u>! The Castle was almost *a vacant shell* with no luxuries of beds; just sparse furnishings and minimal foods and water...The Mandolins were *so angry*! Once again they had been outsmarted! Antoine ordered his men to set up camp right outside the Castle walls while he and his top soldiers set up their camp *inside*!

Once again, they were startled to *hear* and *see* for themselves the same *chaos* happening around them all over again! While some slept; others who were *on guard* watched as their weapons, horses and food *magically disappeared*! They shot arrows 'into the air' and *clubbed* at *nothing* and were only getting more frustrated and angry even at each other; *their tempers flaring*!

This time their leader did not bother to replace the horses; they set up camp with more men outside the walls surrounding King Williams Castle; knowing they could drug their food or drink – they <u>did not eat nor drink</u> but tried to stay awake and closely kept watch!

Antoine's men were beginning to *get tired* and hunger was beginning to set in! The following morning some of his followers already started to *abandon him* and his league!

They also realized that without the Healing Faeries help and influence in the Peoplefolk Kingdom that their *families and friends* who depended on the herbs and 'healing remedies'; were also suffering along with them!

Word got out once again that the Captain of the Mandolins wanted to meet with King William and Prince Davey! But the Prince and King William were wise to his dealings and sent four of King William's men to set up a place and time to meet! And if *things got out of hand* his men were to abandon the effort and use their **POWER** to *disappear* if need be!

In the meantime Queen Isabella had gone to France *through* the Faery Realm to *speak* and *plead* with Prince Ivan to come home; they needed every bit of help for *all to unite* to save the future of the Healing Faeries and to keep their *FREEDOM;* they so much *believed in*!

When Isabella arrived she was in a *state of frenzy*! Immediately Prince Ivan gathered his Queen Mother, Emilie, Gabriel, Cecile and his top warriors to meet in the great room! They were all shocked with the grave news that Isabella had brought to them; *especially* the Queen Mother! She did not hold back her tears of *anger and sorrow* for the plight of her dead Husband, their Kingdom and Isabella's Kingdom of the Healing Faeries! But she *was* very thankful and grateful that Isabella was able to *fly through the Faery Realm* this *quickly* to warn them! Their admiration for Isabella grew that day as she stood proud and tall in front of them; beautiful, *courageous* Isabella dressed in her battle clothing; the Queen of the Healing Faeries *coming to their aid* and having to *share* the latest *grueling* tale of events!

"I cannot tell you enough how hard our warriors are fighting in the *INVISIBLE REALM* for our people and *yours!*" she stated firmly. "But now we need your help; your forces, your men and your *courage* Prince Ivan to complete us and to try to put *an end* to this ongoing battle once and for all!" she added. "Our people have been intertwined and have lived side by side for so long and now we know this runs deeper than the Mandolins *wanting our lands!*"

"Aye, your Grace," answered Prince Ivan, "I see I have proved myself wrong and have acted *foolishly and selfishly*; for all the wrong reasons! I do an injustice to you and your people and my family and our Peoplefolk; I am *ashamed!*" he added sadly; heartbroken about the news of his Father being *murdered!*

"Aye, well *now* is the *TIME* for you to come to our aid and use every bit of your strength to make things *right* for your Brother and your *FATHER!*" Isabella replied in a courageous tone!

It was then that Queen Ivy asked Jenny her longtime servant who had travelled with her and *been through all things with her* to please fetch something *stronger* than tea for her guest and all those in attendance; it was time to 'battle it out' and to sort out and lay on the table *everything* each one of them could think of 'why' this was happening to them!

They all came to agreement that night that it was indeed on a *personal level* and seemed more like a vendetta which had brought on such hatred to go so far as to *murder* King Rennie!

That night in the Great room where they had spent several hours in; it was not like them to be in such duress, but there were dirty dishes; half emptied drinks, food and papers all strewn about and everyone oblivious to it all; everyone, *except Isabella*! It was about midnight that Isabella stood up and told them to gather around closer; she was *ready* to make her *final announcement* to them! Tiredly, everyone shifted around so they could *hear* what she had to say...

"It is hard to find the *right words* at this time to let you know the *extremities* of what I may have to do;

having been instructed by my *own Father* and King Rennie about this very thing, thinking *innocently*, I shall never have to use it; I now find I have *NO CHOICE!* We have to leave on the morrow', as soon as possible; gather all those to us for there is 'no time to spare'! We have to go back to *Scotland*; we shall meet at Nanny Belle's *old cottage by the bluff* – a place you all know! *There*; I will tell you *our fate!*" Isabella said as she stood up. *Abruptly*; she left the room without a backward glance!

Although it was late into the evening Prince Ivan gathered his *own* men and had his *own meeting* in the larger study down the hall. There was much to do and they planned to work *late into the night* to get it done!

Isabella, Emilie and Queen Ivy planned to stay in the same quarters that night spending nay' a sleepless night *perhaps* but at least they were together; no one knowing the outcome or if they would see one another again!

Emilie planned to leave with Isabella in the first *light of day!* Cecile was to stay with the Queen in France where the Queen Mother would be *safe!* Prince Ivan and all others who were not of the *Faery Realm* had to set sail *at dawn*! *Luckily* they lived close to the water!

Before saying *goodnight* Queen Ivy came to see Isabella bringing 'gifts' she had made for her... "I have been kept busy sewing and knitting Isabella and I have made you some *doilies* for you to take back with you which *match* the shade of your blue in your eyes' and a warm shawl I had made for you; in *our Clan colors*!" she said quietly. "I want you to know you are like a Daughter I have never had and *I love you dearly*! I would have liken you to have perhaps *gotten together* with one of my Son's *but now* I am glad you chose your William; your loyal, devoted, *brave* William!" she added as she hugged Isabella to her. Isabella looked down at the blue and white handmade treasures and the purple and green plaid shawl! The *motto* for the Queens Scottish plaid meant; *FREEDOM* which suited Isabella and her Clan in *every way*!

"Thank you your *Highness* - Mother Ivy!" she said as she held them to her breast, "I will treasure them as a bond of our love' and will carry one of them closest to *my heart* in my battle clothing' as I make my Healing Faery *warrior stance!*"

"God bless you Lass!" said the Queen as she bid goodnight' and layed a kiss upon Isabella's brow. "King Rennie would be *so proud!*" she added before she disappeared into the bed chamber!

Isabella went to find Emilie and to make preparations for bed! She was so proud that Emilie had *agreed* to go to Scotland and fight for her right to be a *HEALING FAERY!* It was a brave thing to do for she had chosen to live 'without wings' among the Peoplefolk for *so long* and now she needed the extra courage to fight not only for *her freedom* but the *freedom of her family*; to do *the same!* Just like the Peoplefolk; in times like these it's 'our family ties' that bind us to one another and the *truth* that sets us *free!*

Emilie also knew the *dangers* involved and wanted to stay close to her son, Gabriel; her husband, Prince Ivan and near Queen Isabella; her *precious niece!* When the Healing Faeries activated their *powers'* and <u>chose</u> to be *WITHOUT WINGS*, walking among the Peoplefolk doing their *healing work*; they knew -

that *every day* they were *at risk* and knew they could face *death* at *any time!*

Isabella's mind was racing as she tried to concentrate on her small tasks at hand! She had to at least try to capture some sleep before sunrise even if only for a *couple of hours!*

Finally after braiding her long hair she crawled into bed; succumbing to her tiredness! At first Queen Isabella tossed and turned but eventually she settled into 'fits of sleep' and started *DREAMING...*

In her dream, she clearly sees her Grandfather Stewart, her Fathers/Father! He was sitting on a bridge near Faery Hill near her *home* in Scotland – the bridge they called; the *Faery Bridge!* She was so happy to see him in her dream for she had loved him so much and was only eleven years old when she had *last* saw him; before he was *killed!*

In her dream she was still the eleven year old 'spoiled Faery Princess' happily *flying* over the bridge to see him! As she got closer she realized he had a *scarlet liquid* running from his chest and Isabella stopped; for she was *afraid!*

He gently told her, "Aye Lass! *Tis' your Grandfather Stewart*; nay not be afraid, for I have come to tell yea that tis' up to you to save us; *save our people*! You know *this bridge* Lass – ever since you were a little Faery Princess and I know you have heard about the Magic Sword through stories and through our Clan's book! <u>*THE MAGIC SWORD IS under us right now*</u>; under *this bridge* and you will have to be brave and *no matter what happens Lass* you will have to get that sword; you will have to *act fast*! Do *NOT* hesitate one second for it could be *too late*! Do you hear me Lass? Do you hear me?" he said in a booming voice over and over. "Open the <u>largest</u> *Amethyst stone* near the handle in the middle to release the *MAGIC*; the 7th *stone*!" Isabella tried to grab at her Grandfather before he faded away – she wanted to know what had happened and why he had died and she wanted to tell him she *missed* him so! So many thoughts ran through her head...When she awoke Isabella had tears streaming down her face...

Finally after a few seconds she collected herself; she got up and washed her face by candlelight; then got *dressed*! She could nay sleep anymore – she had to be awake, *alert* and *ready*! She had to stay *focused*!

63

While she was getting dressed she took out her Clan's book from its *hiding place* inside her large leather pouch she carried with her! She held it by the candles light and found a poem about the *famous sword*! Her Clan's book was covered with dark purple velvet; worn and *tattered* and inside the intertwined pages bound together with leather ties. It was filled with stories, poetry, their Faery Creed and pictures depicting the Healing Faeries lineage of history; their *way of life*! There were only so many of *such books* left which were handed down through the ages; so they were *sacred*!

She wanted to 'read the poem' for herself while everything her Grandfather had told her in her dream; was *still fresh*! There beside the poem was a *drawing* of the sword; the drawing was faded by time but you could still see the extraordinary detail still on it.

THE SACRED SWORD

IF you are reading my words
WE will know that all has gone amiss
THE *DAY OF THE SACRED SWORD*
IS about to share her kiss... (*Of death*)

NOT many hands have held this *SWORD*
AND none shall do again

ONCE the spell has been let loose
THE MAGIC DUST SHALL settle

AND all those within the FAERY REALM
SHALL nay' be SEEN AGAIN...
ALONG with the Magic sword
With its *ancient sheet of metal!*
*(The death is *symbolic* of: *leaving some way of life; never to return*)

As Isabella stood there holding the book in her hands; her hands were shaking and her breath was coming in *shallow gasps,* as though she were going to *faint*! Every fiber of her being was being *tested*! She knew what could happen and yet reading the words made it so much more *daunting* for her! She put the book back and wiped her face once more with the *cold* water from the stone bowl! She must pull herself together; *NOW*!

Next, Isabella slowly made her way down to the Mansion's main kitchen to get some *tea* and immediately the servants, who were readily available, doted on her! They *remembered* her from her last visit; when she and Gabriel had been in France and *they adored her*! The servants made Isabella feel *more at ease* and with the warm tea her fear dissipated briefly, for a time...

It was if by *chance* though that she met Gabriel upon leaving the warmth of the large kitchen; he was coming down the hall for he too was unable to sleep and woke up early!

Amazingly, he shared with Isabella a *dream* he had during the middle of the night, *"Isabella*, our Grandfather came to me and told me I had to *help you*! It was all in *a haze*; something about a *Faery bridge* – and for me to help 'bridge the pieces' together and something about my 'lucky horse shoe' that I always keep by my side... You know, the one Grandfather gave me?" Gabriel asked; as he brought it out of his cloak pocket; then he added, "He also told me I had to get King Roy to *leave* Prince Edward Island; it was *time* for my uncle, your Father, to *return to SCOTLAND!*"

Isabella was dumbfounded! With all her 'Faery knowing' Queen Isabella *still* did not know how such *miraculous things* happened! "Once again Gabriel we are *intertwined* in togetherness and bound together with our *family ties'*; our lives so *closely woven* – so you must go get *my Father* and tell him we need him in Scotland *right away!*" she said as she watched his blue eyes searching hers for any *telltale signs* of the *'FAERY KNOWING'; stirring within them both!*

"Aye Isabella, I shall leave *right away!*" he answered knowing the *urgency* of every move they made now... He hugged Isabella close and kissed *both her cheeks* and said, "Till we meet again cousin!"

"I *love thee Gabriel* like my own brother I never had and I THANK thee *from my heart!*" Isabella added with tears in her eyes!

"And I love thee like a *SISTER!*" he answered. They were very close and bound together for life; almost like twins - from their time on Prince Edward Island, in France and *especially* now...

Isabella watched and *heard* the Faery chant in her *own head* as Gabriel *disappeared* right before her eyes...

> Spin your dream as though with thread
> Spinning Spinning, round your head
> Chanting and Spinning
> Spinning and Chanting
> Round and round ye go...

After Gabriel left she met up with Emilie and for some strange reason which she did not know yet – she told Emilie where Gabriel had gone and about their *dreams* and she asked her if she could go on to Scotland *ahead of her* and *meet her* at Nanny Belles cottage! She told her she was *fine* – she just needed some more time before she left! Emilie *trusted* Isabella's *intuition*; so she left right away!

After Emilie left it seemed that 'all of sudden' she felt this sudden *urge* to go out into the courtyard to take in the breathtaking *scent* of the *Lavender* to *soothe* her spirits! It not only grew plentiful in their gardens but in the fields *surrounding* Prince Ivan's Mansion!

While she was out there she closed her eyes and as she breathed in the *fresh scent* of the Healing Faeries most *favorite healing herb*, her Faery senses started *tingling*; but 'not in a good way'! She suddenly turned around and thought she saw; in the corner of her eye someone near the *garden wall*!

Suddenly using her Faery ways she quickly *disappeared* and flew over by the trees along the wall...There standing before her; looking all around was *the mystery servant girl* from Scotland; *LILY*! Isabella quickly came up beside her and *reappeared* in front of her; *startling her*!

Stunned the girl started to run but Isabella had time to grab her sleeve! "Wait or I shall call the guards!" Isabella shouted. "So it is *YOU*!" cried Isabella. "Your name is *Lily – the girl* from the Castle Rockland!" she added in a *shocked* voice!

"Why would you *call the guards* Madame!" she said in her French accent as she tried to pretend she was *innocently* just walking through the courtyard gardens.

"Oh, you *cannot* fool me! *Why* would you ever do such a thing – to *MURDER* King Rennie?" Isabella asked; not afraid to show her emotions; not able to *hold back her tongue*! Isabella wanted some answers and she wanted them right away!

"I do not care about your *stupid* King – his son killed *Antoine's Father* and that is all I care about!" she said; showing no fear whatsoever to Isabella. "He was sick anyways and I did him a *favor*!" she added.

"He was too rich and did not care for the poor or for anyone but *himself*!"

"*Oh* you are so wrong!" Isabella said hastily; *angrily.* "What are you talking about? *Which son* killed his Father?" Isabella asked still holding onto her arm!

"*Prince Ivan!*" Lily answered. "It was during *the last war* in Scotland! To think I almost worked *for you* in your Castle Heatheren and if it were *not for Antoine* I would have! You see, his Father killed *your Grandfather* and in turn Prince Ivan killed *Ramón!*" she added not holding back any words!

Isabella stared at her not able to even *answer* back right away! She knew she should call the guards right away and now knew with this information she should *scream* and *cry* and *shake* this French girl! She could do neither; for she was still in <u>shock</u> and wanted to know more...

"What are you doing in *France* – do you *not KNOW* what is happening in Scotland?" Isabella asked. "*YOU* have *started a new war!*"

"My Antoine told me to come to France and wait for him! I am to have *land*, a *title* and a *Castle* for myself in Scotland when I return he said!" she added. "And my name is *not* LILY it is *Paulette*! Don't you recognize me?" she asked.

"*What*? What are you talking about?" Isabella asked the mere conversation shocking her more and more as this French girl shed more light on this whole horrid nightmare which was now going on *at this very moment*; in her homeland of Scotland!

"I met you here *in France* when you were helping the poor and *I too* followed you to Scotland; I went there for your crowning and was there the *day* you *became Queen*! That is where I met Antoine! He told me not to work for you as you kept company with the Peoplefolk King and Queen; who did not share their *riches* with others!" she added breathlessly.

Neither of the women noticed the heavy rain that had started showering down upon them that fateful morning; both were unafraid and *stubborn*; with no care of the weather!

Isabella felt no *victory* and yet here she was with the *most important milestone* of a miracle right before her shedding not only light on *the start* of this war' but the ugly drawn out *TRUTH* of every detail they *needed to hear*!

"Well I want you to know something PAULETTE or *Lily* or whoever you are... Because of *your starting this*; we have had to *fight* using *our powers of the Invisible Realm*!" Isabella stated flatly. "Right now as we speak; *your Antoine* is *hungry* and *tired* for we have repeatedly taken his horses, his food *and* his weapons *secretly* from under his men and his nose while they slept using our *sleeping medicines*! Right now *all peoples* are suffering without the Healing Faeries *healing remedies* and Antoine is *losing* his followers because of it!" she added angrily.

"*Non* – I do not *believe it*!" she said. "Well Antoine said if Prince Ivan did become King - he would be the next to be *murdered*! He will not stop till he *avenges* his Father's death! He is also *friends* with the *King's Sister* and her husband! How do you think we got this far?" Paulette asked as she stood there; still *defying* Queen Isabella!

"I cannot tell you how wrong you are about King Rennie and his Royal Family! They fought on the side of the Healing Faeries back then and now they *still do*...You will not be getting any *Castle* or *riches* when we are done *my dear girl*! It is over! WE are heading back; all of us, today, to *FINISH* this off once and for all and if you wish to continue to help your Antoine *you too* shall find yourself more hungry and even more *impoverished* than you have ever been, *in your life*!" said Isabella in a threatening tone.

It was then that Paulette *disappeared* right before Isabella's eyes! Isabella stood shivering in the rain – *reeling* in the raw *truth;* not only had she *been right all along* about Paulette being *a Healing Faery* but *NOW;* she had just *let her escape*!

The Queen of the Healing Faeries stood there with eyes closed; rain mixed with her tears as she cried 'out in anger' and *pent up feelings* she had held in for *so long*! She cried for her people, for King Rennie; for herself and her Grandfather Stewart whom she *missed* so dearly! "Why was it up to her?" she thought. "Why was it *HER destiny* to have to *avenge* and fight and do what *no other* had done?" And this was *the least*

73

of it all; what *may happen* coming up 'tore at her heart' – knowing that her DREAM will *not* be coming TRUE – *not in the way she had wanted*; not in the way she had *dreamed it to be*...and not 'how it could have been'! Yes; Isabella stood there and cried for *all she believed in* and *more*!

Isabella did not have any more energy left or *time to waste* on her self-pity; she had *her answers* and now she must quickly speed up her *DESTINY*!

Right now Queen Isabella had the *plight of both KINGDOMS* at her doorstep; *the Kingdom of the Healing Faeries and the Kingdom of the Scottish Peoplefolk!* Enough of this crying she thought, "I have to gather all my strength and courage for I am *Isabella, Queen* of the Healing Faeries; the bravest one of all!" she thought bitterly! "And to think Queen Ivy's own sister-in-law had befriended these people!"

And with that thought Isabella opened her pouch and took out her Amethyst necklace her Mother had given her and her KEY of *FREEDOM* and *put them on*! She had taken them off when she had dressed in *trousers* and clothes suitable of 'that of a warrior'!

She was ready to fight beside her people! No dresses or fanfare of a *Queen*; <u>*on this day*</u>! But she would put on her treasures of hope, faith and *gifts* that others had given her for the sheer 'energy' bond that *love bestows*! It was then that Isabella remembered a Faerie poem she knew from the Healing Clan book - which she knew off by heart called; *The Healing Faeries*! It was times like these that *poems* and *thoughts* come into your *mind and heart* to edge you on; to give you *hope*!

The Healing Faeries

We are the *Healing Faeries*
We are the ones that *sing*
We believe in *freedom*
No harm to anyone
We may be *small* we may stay *tall*
We may just *disappear*
But when you *need us* most – *just know*
That we are always near
We're like the wind, the earth, the sea
Just like the skies above
You will *sense* that we *are there*
For you will *feel the love...*

First, Isabella went back into the mansion tell the others about the *TRUTH* she had just learnt; from Paulette! She also instructed Cecile to use *every ounce* of her Faerie powers to detect if *Paulette* has returned; to protect themselves and *Queen Ivy*!

Entering into the Faery Realm, Isabella then flew to the ship they called the Alabaster to *warn* Prince Ivan and his men! Time was of *the essence*; she had to get help from the Healing Faeries to capture Paulette and 'share this discovery'; *this treason* from one of *their OWN* kind! Soon they *all would know* what a tangled web this has turned out to be! Far more tangled than they had ever imagined and it was *TIME* to put a stop to *this insanity*! This was the last thing that she wanted surrounding the Healing Faeries and what they stood for; what they *believed in*!

The winds had shifted and when Isabella arrived on the ship the rains had stopped and you could smell the old wood, the dampness and the smell of *old* lamp oil! The ship rolled and heaved as the large waves from the storm thrashed it about!

Isabella *reappeared* and immediately recognized one of Prince Ivan's men on the deck!

"Bonjour, Oliver – it's *Queen Isabella!*" Isabella said softly - so not to startle him and cause him to reach for his sword; *in haste!*

"*Queen Isabella!*" he said slowly taking his hand off his *sword*...Then making a rugged form of a bow; in jest, he asked, "What has happened, *Mon Cherie?*" Oliver asked in *his gruff voice* as he watched her ashen face; full of desperation; dance *in and out* of his view as the full moon fought to appear from beneath the clouds *lighting up her face* and *the darkened deck!*

"Oh Oliver, I need to warn *Prince Ivan* – we have to be on alert!" she answered trying to speak louder to be heard above the winds and the rolling waves! "You have to be aware of a *pretty raven haired girl* – she has got to be captured for *TREASON; for the murder of KING RENNIE of Scotland! She goes by the name of Paulette!*" she added.

Behind her she heard a *sharp intake* of breath and then a voice she *recognized*, "ISABELLA!" Prince Ivan called out to her! He grabbed her by the arms and said, "What are you doing here? You are supposed to be back in *Scotland* by now!" he said not waiting for a response... "You have talked to the *girl* Isabella? She was in *FRANCE*?" he asked as he shook her arms trying to make her speak! "Isabella, *tell me!*"

"Yes, Yes!" Isabella finally said *snapping out* of her *dazed* state! "You have to be careful Ivan; she is a *Healing Faery*; she can be anywhere – please, please; be careful what you *eat or drink*!"

"Isabella I will make sure we capture her and I will warn my men; *Oliver* will help me!" he answered hugging her to him! "I am sorry if I *hurt you*...Please tell me Isabella - *where is Emilie*? She is supposed to be with you; is she alright?" the Prince asked.

"I have sent her to Nanny Belle's, *without me*! I had to come and *warn you* and now I must be on my way!" she said hurriedly.

The Prince hugged her once again for he was so grateful to her for so many things and in *times like these* no one knows the outcome; it could be the *last time* they see one another!

But he stopped her before she left, saying, "Wait! *Please* give this to Emilie!" as he gave her something in her hand... Isabella looked down at the pouch and back up at Prince Ivan... "It's a lock of *Emilie's hair* she gave me when we first met on Prince Edward Island – *keep it safe* till we *all* meet again!"

"Aye, you can count on me – BE SAFE! `Au Revoir, *Mon Ami*! À la procaine!" Isabella answered. *Within seconds* – Isabella disappeared into the Faery Realm! She had just said 'goodbye in French' and till they speak again; they will *part ways*!

When you are *within* the *Faery Realm* it does take time to get to places which are *further away* but when you are within that 'magical dimension'; it feels like it has just been *seconds, like a BLINK OF YOUR EYE!*

ISABELLA IN SCOTLAND PART III

The Faery Bridge – Castle Heatheren –
The Magic Sword – The Scroll

PART III

While Isabella had been gone; their situation in *Scotland* had deteriorated! The herbal remedies of the Healing Faeries were no longer available and you could sense a lack of *well being* everywhere!

But that wasn't the feeling as she passed over the hills *leading* to Nanny Belle's cottage! When Isabella arrived by the old stone walls, surrounding the cottage – it looked like a 'bustling little town' had taken over her vacant property! There were caravans, tents and multiple campfires; it was night and even though they were going through *strife* there was *merriment* about! There were tin whistles and campfire songs still going on...

Nanny Belle's familiar cottage and barns were surrounded by *beautiful stone walls*; the *very garden walls* where William and Isabella had dug up her necklace; her 'key of freedom' that was buried there! It seemed like so long ago; but now - only yesterday as she stood there taking in the scenes around her!

"Oh - how things have changed so since that *innocent time* in our lives!" she thought. Isabella flew around in the 'Invisible Realm' as she sought out to find William, Emilie, Nanny Belle and the others!

Isabella found them in the cottage; they had gathered some makeshift furniture and you *could tell* they had all pitched in to make it reasonably *comfortable* for the time being! Isabella suddenly reappeared in front of them by the old stone fireplace; to all their astonishment! They had been *so worried* about her when Emilie had showed up; *without her*!

William was the first to grab her and hug her to him! *Then* Nanny Belle and Emilie!

"Isabella, I was so *worried* about you!" cried William. "Look at you; what happened?" William asked not waiting for an answer, "Your eyes *are red;* like you were *crying!*" he added, as he took notice of her *damp* clothing and her half braided hair!

"Sit down Isabella, sit down child!" cried Nanny Belle as she poured her some Lavender tea! "William, let her tell us what has happened and take your time *my Darling*!" she said soothingly; as her own *Mother* would have done!

"Lily; I *mean Paulette* showed up in the courtyard gardens just before I left – *her real name* is Paulette!" she said breathlessly.

"Go on," said William. "Did she hurt you, are you alright Isabella?" he asked with concern rising within his voice.

"No...not in a *physical way* William!" she answered. "But what she revealed to me makes my blood boil *and* curdle!" she added. "Oh my dear family – she did *kill the King* and is <u>happy</u> about it all – she was in Scotland the <u>very day</u> I was *crowned Queen;* that is where she *befriended* Antoine! She even followed me all the way from France after Gabriel and I had been there reuniting with Emilie and working *to help the poor*! She even worked for our cause!" explained Isabella. Isabella put her head down in her arms and cried softly; unabashed as she continued...

"That is not the hardest part..." she cried, "Antoine is *avenging* his *Father's death*! His FATHER killed Grandfather Stewart and in turn Prince Ivan *killed his Father*!" she stated as her face tilted up to see the faces of those surrounding her! "And that is why King Rennie was *murdered!*" she cried out.

"Oh Isabella!" cried Nanny Belle.

"No!" cried Emilie. "*My* Ivan killed *his Father*? His life is in danger –all this is for *REVENGE*?" she asked looking back and forth at each one of them!

"Isabella so what happened; where is the girl *now*?" William asked; concerned for the safety of his Queen!

"William - *she DISAPPEARED!* I was *right*; she is one of us, she is a *HEALING FAERY*!" she said desperately. "*I let her escape* and *now* she could be anywhere so I flew' to the ship and *warned Prince Ivan!*" she added.

"Oh, Mon Dieu!" cried Emilie!

"The TRUTH must be told now my Isabella! There is no turning back! We must search out Antoine and his men; whoever is left and *finish this*!" he added as he bent down holding Isabella in his arms rocking her back and forth. "You must get some *REST* my Queen; for our 'day of reckoning' is coming!" William said.

"Hear, Hear!" said Nanny Belle and Emilie in *unison* as they stood in the background watching; their hearts 'filled with love', for their *brave Queen Isabella*!

Before William took Isabella to bed, Isabella wanted to finish filling in the last of the details of *how* Antoine had *met Paulette*; and the *promises* he had made her to *encourage* her to his side; to go to such *lengths* to murder; to fight - *his* battle!

"Before I retire for bed I just wanted to tell you *WHY* Paulette has done this *horrible deed*!" Isabella said as she gathered them all together again. "Antoine *KNEW* she was a HEALING FAERY so he befriended her and introduced her to *of all people*; King Rennie's sister and her husband who she *admitted* are in on the whole scheme! Now we know just how *deep* their interests were in wanting to find out about their *monies* and their *worth*! *Antoine* also promised Paulette riches; a title, lands, her own Castle and *she believed him* <u>and</u> *fell in love* with him!" she added feeling almost *sad* for the girl now as she shared it with her family!

Nanny Belle was the first one to speak, "Oh, my Isabella I cannot even think of how you felt; hearing *all this* alone! I am so saddened by the reason for *all this tragedy*; for love and money and greed!"

They all hugged Isabella to them and shared their love for one another openly for they knew Queen Isabella needed her rest to *continue* on this journey - that was by no means *over*!

Once Isabella was *safe in bed* and William knew she was asleep; he went to talk to his family by himself. Then he went to brief his Clan members with the latest news knowing this was indeed going to be a *long* night!

It took *more* than two days for Prince Ivan and his band of men to arrive by ship; the weather had been foul and had slowed them down! When he arrived he was so glad to see *Emilie* there and that they were *all safe*! He had such horrible thoughts in his mind on the journey over by ship! Now they just needed to wait for Gabriel to arrive with *hopefully*; Isabella's Mother and Father!

They did not have long to wait; while they were busily gathering up their men, *securing the hideout* at Nanny Belle's cottage and making their preparations on how to *capture Antoine*; they *appeared*!

There was such a 'rush of *happiness*' for them all at the sight of *brave handsome* Gabriel leading King Roy and Queen Eve straight into the arms of *their* blood relations; the most beloved of all; *FAMILY*!

Isabella ran to them *first*! The sight alone of seeing her glorious tall rugged handsome Father; *his long grey wavy hair - his trademark* as always unruly and *blowing in the wind*! And as a *true Patriot* of the Healing Faeries there was a *certain trait* which held them apart. They wore one long braid to the *left side* of their face which trailed down closest to their *heart*!

Her *Mother*, Queen Eve seemed not to have changed at all; she looked *just as beautiful* as Isabella had last saw her; *two years* ago! Her long red hair was piled up high with one long loose braid coming down and she he too was not dressed in *her usual finery* but had on a rugged woolen cloak made not for looks; but for *warmth*! Oh, but she had on her *plaid colors* draped across her cloak; the *soft blues* matching her vibrant blue eyes! They all took turns showing their affection mixed with heartfelt messages and *glad tidings*!

It was starting to get cool; *so much time* had gone by; the weeks rolling by, the *seasons* changing just as fast as 'the tides of their future' - *they were riding on*!

As quickly as possible, Isabella and William brought her parents inside Nanny Belle's makeshift cottage for some warmth, tea and some broth they had made; anything to ward off the *chill in the air*! They also wanted to talk to them *privately* about the latest TRUTHS; the animosity and the *mayhem*!

Gabriel, Emilie and Prince Ivan were also glad for the chance for them to *unite once again* and later they went off to Prince Ivan's *caravan* to sit by the fire and to share their feelings now that everything was *OUT* in *the open*! No one wanted to speculate what the outcome would be for no one *really knew*...

The *only one* that was missing was Prince Davey! He had gone with his men to gather up some more horses, soldiers *and food*! At this point in the Peoplefolk Realm *and* the Faery Realm – royalty, notoriety and anarchy were almost *removed* as each one of them worked *side by side* with their people; not *above* them!

That *night* was one of the best nights they all had in *a long time*! Prince Davey and his men had arrived just before dusk which made their close knit family ties – *complete*! They were the ones who had stood by one another; the ones *left* to *finish the fight*!

There was no denying that Gabriel was missing Cecile and they all missed the *Queen of the Peoplefolk* who they had come to *love*! But they were safe in France; *for now*! So Gabriel played his tin whistle to keep his mind off his loved one and the others sang and kept *warm* by their fires!

They all had been through so much and the 'bond of love' was so strong for all of them – they all felt in a *joyful and thankful* mood! Prince Davey and his Brother got to *reunite* under these circumstances and they also felt that 'brotherly bond' they had when they *were much younger*! They stayed close together that night and Prince Ivan was pleased to find out that his Brother had been *busy* for he had had recently *fallen in love* with Rosetta; Isabella's friend and servant and now; he was not *alone anymore*! They *both* seemed very happy in these most trying times and they made a *lovely* couple!

Those closest to Queen Isabella were invited into the cottage later that night for a more *private gathering*; the cottage felt indeed 'a lot smaller' than when Isabella had once lived there with William and Nanny Belle for that brief year; so many years ago!

There was much laughter, singing and *storytelling* that night...It was as if *nothing* were going on; they all seemed to just stay in the *MOMENT* with each other and that was a very *GOOD freeing* thing! It felt like the way things were *way before* anything had changed in the *Kingdom* – and that was a feeling that would stay with each one of them; in all their *hearts*, *FOREVER*!

But along the coast of Scotland there was a *different scene*! During this time of 'gathering' for the Healing *Clan* Antoine had been busy realigning with more recruits and gathering strength with robust young lads who were swayed again with; talks' of *riches*

and rewards! Antoine did not *listen to* the rumors of people starving and suffering without the 'healing remedies' or care about the outbreak of *unruliness* throughout the Kingdom with <u>*no KING on the throne*</u>!

His *greed* was fiercer now than ever and he thought he was *unstoppable*!

As fate would have it; on the very *night* of Isabella's *happy* gathering, *Paulette* had caught up with Antoine and had told him she had talked with Queen Isabella in France and he was <u>*furious with her*</u>! "Why would you even talk to that *Faery witch*!" he said in anger as he jumped down off his horse. "I told you to *stay in France* and what was Isabella *doing in FRANCE*?" he asked as his voice echoed, in among the groups of tall pine trees!

"Stop *shouting* at me Antoine, s'il vous plaits!" Paulette cried. "I need to talk with you; *alone*!" she answered. Antoine's men and horses were uneasy with Paulette's *surprise visit*! The Mandolins *did not like her* or feel comfortable with her; nor did they trust her even though she had killed *King Rennie*!

But she was a strong girl and she did not flinch from the animosity she felt from them!

"Make it *quick!*" Antoine said.

"Antoine; are things as *bad* as Queen Isabella said?" she asked as she looked up at him. "Are people starving and missing the healing ways? What have you *DONE?*" she added; *still wanting answers*!

"Why do you care, Paulette?" he laughed bitterly. "They will *recover,* we are *ahead* now – we will keep going till we *destroy* <u>every last one of them</u>!" he added. "We have gathered riches along the way, hidden our *food source* for ourselves and we will continue to do so – just ask my *fine MEN* that *ride by my side!*" he jostled with conceited benevolence; *loud enough* for his men to hear!

"Hear! Hear!" was heard as a reply in *unison* by some of his so called; *fine men*! Paulette looked around at their greedy faces; his soldiers now a mix of older experienced *felons* and *misguided youth* with no path; *no future* but to join a band like the MANDOLINS! Their angry sneering faces stared at her like a 'piece of meat' ready to be *eaten*! Paulette shivered...

"Antoine, *you have gone too far* – they have used their *invisible force* on you!" she said. "*They* too will not stop!" she said forcefully.

"Are you getting *cold feet* Paulette?" he asked her. "Maybe you should go join your *OWN KIND* and leave us men to finish this fight!" he added as he *rudely* spat on the ground beside her!

"*Non!* You do not *mean* that Antoine!" she said slowly searchingly looking up at his rugged handsome face; into his piercing dark blue eyes. "I *love you*; we were going to be *together*; you *promised me* Antoine!" she pleaded. As she looked up at his face she was shocked at the stony silence and telltale signs of *hatred* as he looked passed her with a look of *impatience*.

"I do not *need you Paulette*; go back to your Healing Faery Clan where you *belong!*" he said without flinching a muscle!

"AYE - but you do *need me* Antoine...for the Healing Faeries are heading this way; I heard they want to meet at the *FAERY BRIDGE* by the Castle Heatheren! They are coming to *GET YOU* Antoine -within the coming days! Prince Davey's' scouts *know* you are still *camped* at the Castle Heatheren!" she cried out!

She did not think it would *end like this*; with her being in the *middle*! No one knew she had been at Nanny Belles' cottage the *night* before! She had stayed in the background and had overheard their plans by *sheer miracle*! When the dogs stirred and one of the Healing Faery *guards* came close to her hiding place she had to flee immediately; so she could go *undetected*!

"WE SHALL BE READY for them and be waiting at the *BRIDGE*! THIS IS FOR *YOUR TROUBLE* – now *get out of here* and *never* come back to see me; EVER! *DO YOU HEAR ME*?" he added in a roaring voice as he through a *leather pouch* filled with coins; at her feet! "You are a *Healing Faery* and everything about you *disgusts me* and *my men*!" he said with vengeance. "Leave or my men will KILL YOU!" he added as he looked back towards his band of Mandolins for *support*!

With one last look; Paulette *disappeared* before them! She did not go far; just out of reach of them -*watching* as they rode back towards the Castle

Heatheren! Paulette could *not believe* what had just happened; making her way over to a lone pine tree she leaned against it; and wept!

"What have I done....*what have I done*?" cried Paulette to herself as she shut her eyes tightly - trying to shut out her thoughts of all the people she has hurt; *in both the lives and future* of the Peoplefolk and the Faeryfolk alike! As the wind blew all around her she opened her eyes pulling her cloak tightly around her feeling the cold reaching deep within *her soul*; she *knew now* what she must do!

Suddenly a pine branch fell off the tree and landed at her feet. Knowing the Healing ways as much as she did; she knew it was *a sign*! Pine means renewal; a burst of freshness and *a chance*; to *begin again*! There was still time to go to Queen Isabella and turn herself in *and* tell them about *Antoine*!

Immediately she headed in the direction of Nanny Belle's cottage! The only reason she knew where it was 'as fate would have it' was her *connection* to Isabella in France. She had worked *side by side* with Isabella and Gabriel when they were in France; she was one of the ones helping feed the poor and leaving the *healing remedies* for the French farmers and villagers! It seemed like so long ago for her! She *had believed* in Isabella and Gabriel's dream *back then*; enough to follow Isabella back to *SCOTLAND!* She had also almost 'fell in love' with *Gabriel* for his good looks and his charm but he had found another love; a girl named *Cecile!* "Why did I let my *heart* rule my *head* and fall in love *with Antoine*?" she asked herself...Paulette had so many thoughts running through her head as she flew' through the *FAERY REALM!*

Luckily, Paulette had found out about Nanny Belle and William and where they had lived just by listening in *on many* of their *intimate conversations!* They took *no notice* of her then; but they *certainly* know of her *now!*

It was *daylight* as Paulette flew' to the stone wall by Nanny Belles old cottage! She was so full of remorse - but time was running out and she needed to face' the TRUTH and *give herself in!*

There were lots of campfires already lit and lots of people about as she arrived at the cottage door! She had *reappeared* and wanted to appear at the door as

Peoplefolk; bravely ready to *accept her fate* at the *hand* of Queen Isabella!

No one was more *shocked* than Isabella when Nanny Belle answered the door; there on the threshold, for all to see was *PAULETTE*! William and Gabriel abruptly stood up sensing something was wrong; never having seen Paulette's *face*!

"PAULETTE!" cried Isabella...

"Qui, *Ma belle Reine!*" she answered bowing before her. "It is I – I *SURRENDER!*" as she knelt down on her knees! "I beg for mercy as I *kneel* before you!" she answered as she *cried* softly into her open hands! All she kept sobbing in French was, *"My beautiful Queen! My beautiful Queen!"*

William looked at Isabella unsure of what to do in case it was a *trap*! He quickly grabbed Isabella and placed her behind his back as Gabriel also recognizing the danger; got in front of her as well to *protect her*!

"*I am alone* – *I beseech you;* I talked *with Antoine* and I am sorry to tell you *I overheard your plans* and I have told him you are going to meet him by the *FAERY BRIDGE* – I did it *out of anger*! S'il vous plaît pardonnez-moi!" Paulette cried; as she *begged* for *forgiveness*!

"You did *what*?" Gabriel was the first to speak – to question her. "*William* – they *know* of our plan!" he said gravely.

"How do we know we can trust you further?" William said, "You are a *MURDERER*!" he added with contempt...

"PLEASE...*BELIEVE ME*!" she screamed as she grabbed his pant legs!

Nanny Belle and Prince Ivan both grabbed for her hands at the same time as she fell into them; like a ragged doll, *sobbing*!

Queen Isabella spoke, "I think she is telling the *truth* but what shall we do now...?" she asked.

"Ma *Reine*!" Paulette cried... "Antoine has *lied* to me – he used me; he said if I did not *leave* him then – his own men would *KILL ME TOO*!" she added as she shouted; my Queen – *in broken English*!

Prince Davey was not in the cottage but Prince Ivan knew that one of them would surely want to *harm this girl* that had killed their *FATHER*; and he did *NOT* want it to be him! He held himself together enough to say, *"I will go and get the guards* and they will tie her up for now; for *our* safety as well as *HERS!"* he said as he stomped by her...

Very quickly, she was taken *prisone*r till they decided what to do with her! She was held captive by *two* of the Healing Faery clan members so if she was *to vanish – immediately* they could go into the Faery Realm and *follow her*! You could feel the tension 'in the air' as the news spread about the camp...

"WE have to *get ready* – let us make up a *backup* plan and *use* the girl!" William said

"What do you *mean* William?" Isabella asked.

"She shall be in the *front row* and if she is telling the *truth;* we will *know it*! I am going to get your FATHER! I will gather our families and start our formation! *IT'S TIME* my Queen!" he said bravely.

Nanny Belle and Isabella hugged William and kissed him before he left the *safety of the cottage*! No one knew what the outcome of this day would be! There was no time for long *good-byes* or *what if's;* now! Prince Davey was furious when he found out the girl was in their camp but there was no time for confrontation; they had a battle to fight; *TODAY*!

William had gathered as many of the Clan together as he could to let them know they would *use* the girl on the front lines since she was the one who started this *with the Mandolins*!

They also decided, in order to *capture* Antoine and those closest to him; they *would not* go into battle in the 'INVISIBLE FAERY REALM' this time but like that of *PEOPLEFOLK*; face to face!

As they doused out their campfires everyone prepared themselves and their horses *for battle*! There was one good thing; they had 'plenty of horses' and *weapons* which they had captured during their first siege from the band of the Mandolins at the Castle Rockland!

As they started lining up in their formations there was an *eerie silence* among them! They had brought as many provisions as they could in case their plan did not work and they had to set up camp near Faery Hill at the Castle Heatheren - later that night!

Isabella and her family rode at the front! They did not hide at the back as some royal families did within the *Peoplefolk Realm*! They were not afraid to fight alongside their *Faery comrades*; this was their last chance for *FREEDOM* and they were willing to go to great lengths for it!

William, Gabriel and Isabella were side by side; then her Father and Mother, Nanny Belle and Prince Davey and Prince Ivan! Paulette was on her own horse but Prince Ivan had a *lead* that attached to his own... Rosetta and Emilie rode just behind Paulette to keep an eye on her! They were also *closely* surrounded by the Faery Clan warriors and the Royal Brigade soldiers. They all rode in *silence* as each one silently thought about their own *loved ones* or speculated the *outcome of it all*...

The *Healing Faeries* had a heightened sense of awareness that set off a 'kind of energy' that attracted birds; small wildlife and elementals that roamed in the woods, the rocky green hills and the glens. Even the earth, the trees, the vegetation and the wild flowers *shared* their *energies* creating a calming, *ethereal* effect!

Unlike the Peoplefolk with *five senses*; the Healing Faeries had *SEVEN* senses! There was; sight, sound, taste, smell, hearing and the sixth and seventh were their ability *to fly*, *disappear and reappear* as Faeries and <u>*materialize as Peop*lefolk</u>; *without wings*!

They also had such a keen sense of hearing; they could hear a human *heartbeat* a *mile* away! The Healing Faeries had 'extraordinary powers' and because of their *values* and *purpose*; tried not to *misuse* them!

They stopped by a large stream just half an hour outside of the outlining property of the Castle Heatheren to water their horses and to take a break before the battle began! They had sent some scouts up just ahead to watch for any *likely ambushes* the Mandolins were known for.

Queen Isabella was to talk to Antoine first and then King Roy; Isabella's Father, *would take over*! They would try to persuade him by using *generous offers of land* and *title* which was still being offered by Prince Davey and his royal family! It could be futile at this point but it sounded as though he was still hungry for *power* and *wealth* of the *material kind* and they could provide it for him if he would *promise* to keep the PEACE and *his part* of the bargain!

While everyone *briefly* lingered about; Queen Isabella and her family *took advantage* by openly showing their affection with one another 'once more' before getting back on their horses; bravely continuing towards the Faery Bridge!

They could see the bridge in the distance now and it was if the 'heavens' knew a battle was about to begin and the dark clouds overtook the sun making the natural beauty surrounding them - look *bleak*!

They were almost to the edge of the bridge when they spotted the Mandolins coming forward themselves in their own formation; the *large* Castle Heatheren looming in the distance, as a backdrop for them.

King Roy signaled for the others to *get ready*! The plan was for QUEEN ISABELLA to talk with the leader *first* and meet him in the *middle* of the Faery Bridge!

It was a *safe place* to talk and meet; a place *to test the waters*! Isabella was instructed if it *did not go well* – she was to *disappear immediately* into the *INVISIBLE REALM*!

When the *Mandolins* saw them stopping on the other side of the old stone Faery Bridge they changed their speed – making haste to get there; their horses pranced and pulled on their leads while the men; like their horses were impatient to get the *fighting started*! Antoine stopped on the other side and yelled over to the Queen; trying to talk above his men!

Isabella could not hear him above the battle cries so she moved forward onto the bridge *about half way* and stood waiting on her horse Gladiator! Antoine was even more handsome than she had heard; even from that distance – she could see his long dark curly hair and see his striking masculine *French features*. The leader held up his hand to quiet down his men to bring some *kind of order* to their *pre-victory stance*!

Queen Isabella bravely sat there on her horse ready to *heed the call* of the Healing Faeries – trying, *ONE LAST TIME* to *reason with* Antoine!

"The Royal family; of the Peoplefolk are *prepared* to allot you lands, titles and the wealth you so strive for *if* you will stop using your *brute force;* to *acquire!* The whole Kingdom is suffering because of you ANTOINE and your *selfishness!* <u>This is your *LAST CHANCE* to change the outcome of this day!</u>" she bellowed in her Scottish brogue; *unaware* that she should watch her tongue and her biting words. Even though his appearance was striking for a woman; his barbarian side was well notarized *in the Kingdom!*

"Well, well!" Antoine said, "If it isn't *the Queen* of the Healing Faeries *right before my eyes!*" he yelled back. "MEN!" he cried out, "Meet the *beautiful* QUEEN; the brave Lass who comes 'to do our *bidding*'! *Cannot* the MEN in your life come <u>to do battle?</u>" he asked sarcastically! The Mandolins started sneering and making rude comments above the *banter* of *battle cries!*

Queen Isabella was not daunted, *"If YOU want things to continue* the way they are the Healing Faeries will *no longer* help you or your people and we shall hide and you will never see us again...or come to your homes or your doors...*Is that what you want?*...It has got to end now or *it will be so!*" Isabella cried out <u>not</u> <u>waiting for his reply</u>! "Tell your men <u>they will regret</u> <u>it</u> and *all of their families!*"

Then Queen Isabella tried talking to *the men herself*! "MANDOLINS!" she shouted, "If you continue to FOLLOW your LEADER he is only here for his OWN RICHES and for his *own* VENDETTA! He has you here today – <u>to avenge HIS FATHERS DEATH</u>! BUT it does not stop there – he also got *his woman to KILL for him!*" she said as she turned and looked towards Paulette who was in the front line watching; waiting, like everyone! *"Please* I beg of you; *you can stop this* now – you do not have to fight *Antoine's battles*! He will *not* keep his promises to you!" she added.

Again the banter of the men got louder and they were getting *impatient*!

Antoine intervened, "Men… *DO NOT LISTEN TO HER!* Paulette was just as *greedy for riches* as I; *to kill for it!*" he said as he laughed! Its Prince Ivan *I want* and I shall get him! Enough of this talking; I will get my wealth *and my riches* and I will get it - *my WAY!* Out of my way Queen Isabella *or you may DIE on your FAERY BRIDGE!*" he added; his voice filled with venom! William started to go *forward on the bridge* but King Roy motioned for him to *STOP*!

"ISABELLA, *DISAPPEAR; <u>NOW</u>*!" yelled her Father in his loud Scottish brogue! Antoine started to *come forward* with his sword and dagger in his hand just as ISABELLA *disappear*ed- leaving her horse Gladiator *in his way*! Antoine scrambled to get around the horse as he started to proceed across the old stone bridge; *unafraid*!

Just at that time *there was chaos* as some of Antoine's men took the Faery warriors and the soldiers of the Royal brigade by surprise; coming *from behind* and attacking them; *on their side* of the bridge!

Everyone reacted at the same time and *the fighting began*; everyone tried in desperation to *watch* each other's *back*! King Roy tried to stay at the front of the line by the FAERY Bridge *waiting for Antoine* to arrive; *knowing* that in the midst of the chaos; *he* wanted *to be the one* to come face to face with their leader; to *avenge* - his <u>own</u> FATHERS DEATH!

Meanwhile Gladiator; Isabella's horse *and* Antoine were heading straight towards Prince Ivan and King

Roy! The long old rugged stone bridge was now *full* of Antoine's riders *following him* trying to get across the bridge; trying *to reach* the *Royal families*!

Queen Isabella knew that when she disappeared she had to make it to the MAGIC SWORD; the ancient metal sword with the seven Amethyst Crystals <u>as soon as possible</u>; *to release* the finest, most powerful FAERY DUST; *ever made*!

Gabriel immediately followed her *under the bridge* and in their *Invisible Realm* he quickly helped her unleash the SWORD from its hiding place and helped her to *pry open* the SEVENTH Amethyst stone; *using* his '*lucky horse shoe*'!

Isabella *reappeared* just in time to see Antoine galloping across the Faery Bridge *heading straight towards her FATHER*! But King Roy was fighting *with his back to him*; trying to *protect her Mother*!

Isabella said *a prayer* and then *quickly* threw both hands up; *holding the sword straight up*; as the Faery Dust *magically sprayed high up into the air* and *in seconds*; came *cascading back down...*

At the same time, almost *as in slow MOTION;* Isabella watched horrified as *Antoine* raised his dagger and threw it into the air *–just as her* Father turned around; *the dagger piercing him straight through the heart!*

At that same instant Prince Ivan and Paulette see this and *both of them head towards Antoine* who had *stopped on the bridge* for a moment, relishing in *his victory;* his MEN coming fast behind him! Paulette gets there first and *suddenly* from under her cloak she produces a long battle sword *she had hidden;* raising it up; with full force; she brings it slashing down *upon Antoine!* Then just *as quickly;* Paulette *using* her side dagger – took her *own life; all* right *before Isabella's own eyes!*

Prince Ivan quickly released her lead and raced back to Isabella's *FATHER* and *pulled* him to the ground on the *Faery side of the bridge;* as he tried to *help him;* Gladiator sped past him heading off into the woods!

Suddenly the whole SKY turned an iridescent purple and the whole FAERY BRIDGE disappeared *before their eyes*! The *whole area* around the Faery Bridge was filled with an *array* of rainbow colors 'almost blinding everyone' forcing them to stop what they were doing; and for *split seconds* they were held in *captivity* and *could not move...*

THEN every one of the Healing Clan was immediately cast into the INVISIBLE REALM!

But it was not *like the FULL REALM* - they were *semi transparent*; you could see them; but you could put your fingers through them like they were a cloud of dust or *like a GHOST!*

The fighting stopped altogether as the all the soldiers and Peoplefolk warriors realized the <u>stark realization</u> that not only was the long FAERY STONE BRIDGE <u>gone</u> but so was *Antoine, Paulette* and *Antoine's men* <u>that were on the bridge</u>; *following behind him!*

Seeing all this; a HUSH came over the Mandolins and they started to back up and retreat – some of the Mandolins were shocked and afraid and they *started to scatter!* All you could hear in the *background* was Isabella's MOTHER crying out, "Noooooooooo! Nooooooo!" as she threw herself down on King Roy's body! King William tried to comfort Queen Eve as he ran to her side!

Prince Ivan was still kneeling; his boots only inches from the 'hole' where the FAERY BRIDGE used to be; his hands bloodstained as he had tried to stop the bleeding of Isabella's Fathers wound; using his plaid tartan! KING ROY was dead! Men lay all around them... There was *no more fighting*; *now*!

Emilie, Gabriel, Nanny Belle, Rosetta and Prince Davey were safe! As they rushed to *the scene* that stood before them they all suddenly saw *Isabella LIGHT up*; surrounded by *illuminating blue and purple light*; the light *shimmering, all round her*! She stood tall in her PEOPLEFOLK *stance* but *with her WINDS SPREAD WIDE*! She never looked *more beautiful* than she did that day!

As Queen Isabella stood there with the Magic Amethyst Sword still in hand; she cried out to all those, who were left, "I DID NOT WANT THIS DAY TO COME TO THIS! FROM THIS DAY FORTH the Healing Faeries will not be *visible* to the PEOPLEFOLK and will go *underground*...Only the Peoplefolk who BELIEVE and have *faith* will be able to FEEL that we are near! In the Invisible Realm we will continue to use our influence and our *healing ways* throughout the

EARTH...*Only then* can *we go on* and be SAFE to do *our HEALING work* and *manifest* good in the world! Go forth and tell others in all corners of the EARTH; <u>OUR KINGDOM will be INVISIBLE</u> and people will NOT know for sure if they are talking to a *Healing Faery* or working side by side with one; for it shall *NEVER* be the same as it was, *<u>ever again</u>*!"

It was then that Queen Isabella *bravely* turned and walked towards her *friends and family...* With her *sword* she touched her FATHER'S body and he *disappeared before them* and then she touched her Mothers shoulder and she did the same *and* then; *<u>every last Healing Faery warrior did the same</u>*! Isabella *disappeared last* leaving a 'shimmering of light' surrounding the place where her FATHER had laid...

The only ones left standing on the edge of the cliff were *Prince Ivan* and his brother; *Prince Davey*! They knew what to do. They had been instructed if *the day of reckoning* had come to this they were to head to the Castle Heatheren right away and *wait for them there*; *praying* they had all survived; to do so!

The Mandolins who were left *staggered away in fear* and unknowingness and it was if the HEAVENS knew this and the *winds* blew and the trees swayed and a *great sadness* crept over the meadows and the glens! The skies stayed the color purple - mixed with dark clouds and... it began to *snow!*

Prince Ivan and Prince Davey went to each other and *embraced* one another and were so glad to know they had made it through the battle and *were alive!* They were *grateful* and *thankful* but very *sad* about King Roy and the sadness of the OUTCOME for the Kingdom of the Healing Faeries and the way of life *as they knew it!*

They now looked around them and the rest of the Mandolins that *had survived* had *vanished* almost as fast as the Healing Faery warriors! No *doubt*; to return home to *their loved ones* and tell them *of the outcome!*

"Let us make haste to the Castle Heatheren, Brother!" said Prince Ivan. He was anxious to see them all and to hold Emilie in his arms once again. He also knew his younger Brother would want to see Rosetta! They both knew they had *decisions to make!* Queen

Nancy Lee Amos

Isabella had told them before they had left Nanny Belle's cottage what would happen if she had to USE the MAGIC SWORD and its meaning for the 'outcome of the Healing Faeries' on the Earth! Not just in SCOTLAND but the *ENTIRE EARTH*! It was the oncoming of the *Winter Solstice* and it would always be a time to remember; that 7th day of DECEMBER!

The Scottish Brothers sped to the Castle Heatheren; the snow and the wind blew as the *purple skies* hung over the land for all to see and *for others* to know the sorrow and the TRUTH of that day and the *vast meaning of it*!

When they arrived; they had to wait for the draw bridge to be let down...The Invisible Realm was still closely watched by the Faery warriors as they recognized the *importance of this day* and would still go to great lengths; more than ever to *PROTECT their privacy* !

As soon as they were within the Castle walls they continued through the vacant courtyard as *the bridge* was once again, pulled up! They first went to the stables to leave their horses and were *surprised* to still see the *Peoplefolk stablemen* who still *remained*

114

loyal to the Healing Faeries! The head stablemen were *Brothers* also and they *embraced* them like comrades for they knew them from the Castle Rockland!

"Prince Davey; Prince Ivan, follow us into the Castle through the *secret entrance* from the stables!" said the oldest brother Daniel.

"Have you seen the others yet?" asked Prince Ivan.

"Aye, we have Sir!" answered the younger brother Donald. "They have instructed us to take you to the main Library; where they are *waiting for you*! They have only just arrived themselves not long ago!" he added.

"Aye, we have known a day *like this may come*; Queen Isabella had *warned us* when she arrived back from the Castle Rockland to *be prepared for it*!" Daniel said. "We were 'afraid for their lives' and are HAPPY they have made it through but sad to hear about the Queen's Father, King Roy!" he added sadly.

"Yes it was a *tragedy* for us all!" answered Prince Davey. "We lost a lot of good soldiers and warriors today!" he added.

They soon came out of a 'tunnel like' hallway and entered a room passing through a *large velvet curtain* which was hanging against one of the Castle walls! The scones *were lit* as the day light was darkening due to the dark skies and gloomy snow coming down outside. There were *eerie* patterns of light dancing on the walls ahead of them.

They soon came to a large hallway leading to the main Library and the head stableman; the oldest Brother knocked loudly on the door; *three times*! The door was opened and there stood King William in his *Peoplefolk stance*! He *embraced both men* unabashedly as he stood aside, to let them in...

Inside at the large wooden table sat all the people they loved and admired; all in the VISIBLE REALM just as they had been before this day had started! There was a rush of chairs moving and people moving to hug and hold one another! They all were an *affectionate* family and did not hold back from showing their emotions openly!

"Oh, *you made it*!" cried Emilie as she held Prince Ivan to her.

"Rosetta!" cried Prince Davey as he rushed to her side.

Gabriel also stood by his Mother's side; ready to embrace Prince Ivan. Queen Isabella went to Prince Davey's side as well. Nanny Belle and William stood by the large stone fireplace and waited; off to the side! Queen Eve; Isabella's Mother sat by her husband's body that was laid out on a large lounge/wooden bed! He was covered with a woolen blanket which was made from the Healing Faeries Clan plaid. Although the Healing Faeries live many years longer than normal Peoplefolk; if they are *killed* in *the Peoplefolk Realm* and are not in their FAERYFOLK state/Faery Realm they can *die* just like the Peoplefolk! They *all* took *many risks* whenever they went between the Peoplefolk Realm and *their OWN REALM*! They all knew it! Now it was up to all the Healing Faeries *in that room* to decide *what life* they were going to choose! And for that matter; *all* the Healing Faeries of the EARTH!

Within the Faery Realm the LAW OF THE MAGIC SWORD was being *passed* right now; all *across the EARTH*!

Queen Isabella sat them down to explain once again what the covenant of the Magic Sword meant for *all of them,* "From this day forward *at the stroke of midnight;* as the Queen of the Healing Faeries the COVENANT OF THE MAGIC SWORD WILL BEGIN! We have SEVEN DAYS till the *stroke of midnight* on the 7th day before we <u>must decide</u> if we choose to *live only* in the FAERY REALM or to *live only* in the PEOPLEFOLK REALM - <u>knowing</u> we can *NEVER* return to the FAERY REALM! If you have NOT CHOSEN by then you will NOT have a choice and you will remain in the INVISIBLE FAERY REALM *forever*! If you have chosen the Faery Realm; you may appear to whomever you want but no more can the Healing Faeries be in the *PEOPLEFOLK form* or *mate with PEOPLEFOLK* ever again! It will be forbidden and you will be appearing in a *'GHOSTLIKE'* state; before them! Not like the Realm now where you can touch and feel and be with someone and *are in the flesh!*" she said as she stopped for a few moments to let the *reality* of the Covenant *sink in.*

"King William and I, Nanny Belle, my Mother and Gabriel have decided to live within the FAERY REALM!" she said as she looked around the room. "As the Queen of the Healing Faeries I shall reign as Queen forever being the LAST QUEEN since I have had to use the

MAGIC SWORD and we have been forced to use these measures to continue our HEALING WAYS!" she added. "Right now as we speak even though it is snowing; plans are being made to rebuild our Faery Castle HEATHEREN II – the wee' Faery Castle where Mother and Father lived at one time and where I grew up in; by the *forest of the PINES*! As you all know we have always had the two REALMS; the <u>*Invisible*</u> and the <u>*Visible*</u> and we also had the choice to look like and *be like* the PEOPLEFOLK as we are *standing here today*! So my dear 'Faery Faith Friends' you too shall have to decide for yourselves!" she added. "I shall leave you now and return to see how you feel about your choices and let you talk among yourselves and then we shall *talk more*! Mother and I shall round up some food and drink for us all with the help of our *LOYAL servants* who have stuck by us and have returned with some of our *necessities*! Nanny Belle wants to help us set up some rooms for the night! We have *six hours* left till MIDNIGHT when *our Covenant starts*!" Isabella said as she got up to leave. William got up to take over for Isabella, as they closed the big doors behind them.

"Gabriel and I shall get more wood and stock the fires to keep us *warm* through this long night! I am hoping you will all stay till mornings light and share this time we have left together!" he said as he got up. "Also Queen Isabella and Mother Eve want to do a *special* 'burial' ceremony *as soon as possible*; *before midnight*! There is a *small chapel* on the grounds and we can go through the secret Castle tunnel to get there. We have some plans that we will *share with you* when we get back! I am sure you have much to talk about; we shall leave you to *give you some privacy*; to do so!" William added as he bowed before them all as he departed with Gabriel by his side!

When they reached the outer hallway it was Gabriel's time to speak. "William in *mornings light* I shall go to get *Cecile* – I *know* she will come with me! That is one good thing; in the Faery Realm we can travel and visit others around the world in the *'blink of an eye'* as Isabella always says!" he added with a *little laugh*.

"Aye, that is for sure Gabriel!" laughed King William. It felt so good to laugh and it lifted some of the sadness! "I am so proud of ISABELLA!" he added. "She was *so brave*; *knowing* it was her *DESTINY* and *knowing all along* it may come to this and what *she had to do* while her *own FATHER* lay dying – she is indeed the most NOBLE of *all Queens;* in all the lands!" he said proudly.

"Aye, she is *indeed!*" Gabriel said. "To think we both had those dreams about our Grandfather Stewart and *it all came true!* I did have to help her open the 7th AMETHYST stone on the Magic Sword and *with my lucky horse shoe*; just like Grandfather said in my dream!" he added with amazement. "And to think William – we all have lost our *Fathers* now..." he added, his voice still lost in thought.

"Somehow I truly believe it is all 'WRITTEN IN THE SANDS OF TIME" Gabriel; as my Mother has quoted, *many times*! Perhaps it is all meant to be right up *till this moment!*" the wise young King added as they headed through the snowy courtyard! "Let us get the Brothers from the stables to help us bring a wagon load of wood – we have a *special request*; a *special burial* to perform!" he added with a brave sense of love for King Roy; filling his heart and soul. It was his request *to be cremated* and they would *respect his request*! "Aye, we have to make haste; there is much to do on this first night before the Covenant begins!" Gabriel added, picking up his pace.

PART IV

On The Road to FREEDOM – RULING LIKE THE WIND

Meanwhile Prince Davey, Rosetta, Emilie and his Brother finally had their chance to talk about *their plans* and what the COVENANT meant *for their lives together*!

"King William and Queen Isabella have given us a choice; to move to Scotland and live in their *Castle Heatheren,* Emilie! I am hoping you will *stay with me* in the PEOPLEFOLK REALM, but I will *understand* if you want to be with Gabriel!" he added in his Scottish brogue; *filled with love* and *understanding.*

"*My place is with you* my Husband! I know Gabriel will do well in the *Healing Faery Realm* and with *his Cecile;* whom I am sure will join him!" Emilie answered. "I would be most *honored* to live in the Castle Heatheren and for us to be back in our *homeland of Scotland!*" she added.

"Also; Queen Isabella said with her lovely insight'- we will *delight* in the beautiful room on the top of

the *first tower* of the Castle; the ROOM FOR THE
FAERIES, with all the small *wee'* Faery houses! That
is the room King William built for Isabella while he
was waiting for her return! She said it could be our
SPECIAL SECRET place for all our families to meet
and for other Healing Faeries to visit!" he added;
knowing how much Emilie, would *appreciate* this!

"Oh Ivan, that is *perfect!*" answered Emilie already
feeling better about their choices.

"What of you Brother?" asked Prince Ivan. "Are you
ready to BE KING?" he asked; not waiting for an
answer he added, "You *deserve* to be the *King* of
our lands and I know you *will reign as our FATHER
did* and bring PEACE and prosperity *back* to our
KINGDOM!" he said his voice filled with *pride and
joy!*

"YES!" said Prince Davey. "I am hoping my Rosetta
will stay by my side and be my *Queen; in our Castle
Rockland!* And *together* we can rule our KINGDOM
with love and *healing ways!* What do you say
ROSETTA?" he added in a joyous, *promising* voice!

"I would have to say *YES like yourself; MY PRINCE!*"
Rosetta answered with a *renewed sense of vitality*
and a joyful youthfulness! It was as if the whole room
took on a *rosy glow* – not only from the big stone
fireplace but it was like the *whole room* lit up filling
them all with warmth, love and a renewed *sense of
enthusiasm* which made them feel happy, *hopeful*
and *filled with JOY!* They all stood up and embraced
one another; talking excitedly while waiting for the
others to return to *share their news!*

No one seemed to notice the other 'little MIRACLES'
that were happening *all around them*; while they
rejoiced in their renewed sense of hope; there in
the corner of the room was a *purple glow* totally
surrounding *King Roy's body!* IT was if *the King
himself* was approving all *of their choices* and was
also *rejoicing* in *their love.* <u>Purple</u> was also the *color*
of the Healing Faeries favorite stone; the *Amethyst*
and the color of *Lavender;* their favorite healing
herb!

Queen Isabella and Mother Eve returned with food
and drink for everyone, which was much needed!
When they arrived they could feel the warmth and

the joy of the others and were *excited to hear* what *choices* they had made!

They had decided that after they ate they would do the memorial service for her Father and as a *Faery* 'twist of fate' had it'; it had turned out to be more of a *'celebration'* at the end of this BATTLE DAY!

As they sat and discussed their decisions; they decided they would *CELEBRATE* her Father's *life* and not MOURN *his death* for he would live on in *their hearts*; *forever*! He was a hero to them all for he had *died* saving his wife, his mate; *Queen Eve*!

It was only *ISABELLA* who saw the *purple light* surrounding her Father that night and she took it *as a SIGN* that everything would be *alright* and that it *truly was* her DESTINY to *continue on* and to look at it; not as an ENDING - but <u>*a NEW BEGINNING*</u>!

King William, Gabriel and Nanny Belle came back 'just in time' to finish the last of the meal and *prepare* for the ceremony! They were happy to hear all the news and they knew that they too could travel back and forth and visit with the *two Brothers* and their loved ones in the Faery Realm. Prince Davey would make a *noble King* and Rosetta a lovely *bride* and *Queen* in the coming months; just *as Isabella did*!

They all wished *Cecile* and *Queen Ivy* could be with them *tonight* but they had *sent Roland,* William's faithful friend through the Faery Realm to tell them the 'outcome of the battle' and that Gabriel would travel through the Realm to get *Cecile - the next day*! Queen Ivy had two choices; to live in her own Castle Rockland or to live with Emilie and Prince Ivan; or she could go between *both Castles* - which would make her *very HAPPY*! Also Prince Ivan and Emilie would have to go back to France to close down their mansion and settle their affairs; within the next few days to come!

After their meal Nanny Belle, Queen Isabella and her Mother got all their *healing remedies* out and *their healing tools* they carried with them! Isabella had wrapped her 'gift' from Queen Ivy *in* with her Crystal stones and incense she carried with her in her leather pouch; she kept tied, around her waist! She had told her she would carry it with her *into battle*; and *she did*!

The men had prepared the 'burial alter' in the courtyard beside the *side door* of the Chapel; which could only be *opened* from the *inside*! It was a sacred place; a <u>healing place</u> made specifically for Queen Isabella. It was here they would have their service for the KING; an intimate setting for *close family members*, only! It was not touched during the encampment of the Mandolins for it had its own *secret doorway*! Inside Isabella had all her 'special' herbs hanging up and a *special alter* with candles and small stone bowls for putting herbs and incense in; *for lighting*!

King Roy had left *instructions* with Queen Eve; if anything were to happen to him just what *his wishes were*! He wanted to be *cremated* and in the *morning* when the sun rose, he wanted his *ashes gathered* and he had 'special requests' for where he wanted his *ashes scattered*; of which Queen Eve would *pass on* to the others!

They all gathered out in the courtyard along with the servants who were left at the Castle Heatheren and *watched* as Queen Eve lit the *first* candle to light *the straw*; of his 'last bed'! It had stopped snowing and the moon had come out to shine down on this scene; on the *7ᵗʰ day of DECEMBER!*

A *lone piper* had started to play the bag pipes for the small group; the sound echoing off the Castle walls in a *haunting lull!* It was Daniel; one of the brothers from the stables who was playing the HEALING FAERIES SONG; *'Believing in Miracles'!* Gabriel quickly took out his *TIN WHISTLE* and played *along with him!*

The heat warmed their faces as they stood back and after Queen Isabella and her MOTHER said a *few words* they departed into the Chapel where one of the servants stood waiting to let them in! It was not till they *were inside* that Isabella *broke down crying;* the haunting music *still echoed* in her ears like the haunting scene of her Father; *turning,* only to get *Antoine's dagger* through *his heart!* Her heart ached for just *one more chance* to <u>change that scene</u>; "If only I had been quicker throwing up the Sword with the *Magic Faery Dust!*" she thought. William stayed by her side and held her as she cried. Gabriel continued playing the tin whistle softly *inside* - while Daniel continued his piping outside the Castle walls; staying with her Father; *till the end!*

Her Mother and Nanny Belle *took over for her* and lit the candles and the *incense* and then; put *Lavender oil* into the small burners they had made!

Once Isabella had settled; she quietly nestled beside William on one of the wooden benches they had there! *Her MOTHER* then began the service!

"My daughter, our QUEEN ISABELLA has been through a lot and as I stand up here tonight I can *only speak* from her FATHERS HEART and tell her how much we *LOVE HER!*" she cried as she looked over to Isabella cuddled like a *small child* beside her brave King William!

"I know this service is about *King Roy*; my husband but I cannot help but go on to talk further of his relationship with Isabella! Isabella was not always like she is today; she has *blossomed* like a *wild rose*; one from our garden, on the shores of Prince Edward Island! She has had to be pushed out of the nest because we KNEW it was HER DESTINY to have to be the one to carry this HEAVY burden that we all face *on this night!*" she added with pride in her voice! "HER FATHER knew all this and so did *his FATHER* and he said just on 'this morn' before we started *our march* into battle; 'Give my daughter' *everything* she wants; please give her *my ring to wear* and my *braid* from *my hair*! She is the most courageous warrior I have *ever known*! She is the most *unselfish, true Healing Faery* I have ever known and *she is my DAUGHTER*! Love HER; *AS I WOULD LOVE HER*! CHERISH HER as I would *cherish* her!" she added *on behalf* of King Roy! "*My Isabella* is the Healing Faerie's last HOPE and *with this COVENANT* we all face tonight it HAS been written in 'THE SANDS OF TIME' that ISABELLA, QUEEN OF THE HEALING FAERIES; SHALL REIGN FOR EVER AND EVER!" *shouted Queen Eve* as her voice faltered; she too broke out *sobbing*!

Nanny Belle went to her first and the others all got up to *embrace* her and then they went in turn; to *Isabella* and *William*!

All you could hear were *soft murmurs* of answers, "Hear, Hear!" as each one of them *embraced* one another and shared their tears of the past; *one last time*!

Everyone went back into the CASTLE with William - except *for Gabriel*; he wanted to spend some time alone with Isabella! Gabriel felt *as close to her* and *her family* as anyone could be; except for being *her Brother*! He had lived with his Grandfather Stewart for three years and then he had lived with Isabella and her family for *four*! Their bond was perhaps *stronger* for what they both had *gone through* and he too was feeling *her pain* almost like that of a TWIN sibling!

Isabella never felt *so much loss* as she did without her *FATHER*! But now she *understood her role* and the role of her people *even more;* the importance of their work and <u>*she had to go on*</u>!

She now looked down at her middle finger at her Father's *ring* her Mother had given her; she still could feel *the presence* of her Father on it! Her Fathers lock of his *long grey braid* was safe in her leather pouch; not that he will come back to them; but as her PEOPLEFOLK friends *believe;* the *strength* and *the eternity of life* stays in the HAIR! Also it will be a reminder of *her Fathers* great courage, *stamina* and *fearlessness* that she too must have in order to *rule in* her new INVISIBLE KINGDOM! She would also be helping those who have chosen to live *in the PEOPLEFOLK Kingdom* by supporting them in *any way she could;* still working *through them* to help others in their Realm! Her *real work* really had just BEGUN!

Letting all these thoughts fall to the wayside she sat with Gabriel; both of them *huddling* in the cold together as the fire in the stone fireplace had almost *burnt out*! Only a few candles remained lit but the *smell* of Lavender oil and Frankincense oil *filled* the small chapel and *filled them* with HOPE and *soothed* their *ruffled wings*! She did not feel much like a QUEEN on this night but it was okay; she was allowed to feel this way after the *length of this ONE day*! They *all* were exhausted from battle and the energy it took to come to this moment! She quietly took Gabriel's hand and said, "Let us go in my BROTHER; we will catch cold out here and we need some sleep; *it is almost MIDNIGHT*!" Arm in arm they walked back through the dimly lit tunnel; entering the secret hallway, back into the *main Castle*!

Nanny Belle and her Mother greeted them in the main *LIBRARY*! They had been waiting up for them and had made sure the servants had kept the fire roaring; filling the big room with *warmth* and *comfort* for them! The four of them hugged one another; sharing their love they *felt* for each other!

They knew that Gabriel's Mother wanted to spend a 'little time' alone with him for she knew he would be leaving for France in the morning; to try to *persuade* Cecile to come back to *Scotland* with him!

It was *after midnight* and their COVENANT *had begun!* Isabella, her Mother and Gabriel knew that they had <u>SEVEN DAYS</u> left till they <u>no</u> <u>longer</u> could be *part of the PEOPLEFOLK REALM* and have the *FREEDOM* that *they had tonight!*

And those like *Emilie* who chose the PEOPLEFOLK REALM had <u>SEVEN DAYS</u> till they *no longer* could be a part of the FAERYFOLK REALM! They would lose *their powers* and not be able to have *their WINGS!* BUT; they still had their HEALING WAYS and their knowledge and could still *live* by the *HEALING FAERY CREED!*

Early the next morning Queen Eve gathered all those who were left to come down to the large *cozy kitchen*; choosing not the big old *drafty* dining area! It was more of a *family gathering*; homey and comfortable with the two large *stone fireplaces* going! There was just a few of them left now –EIGHT to be exact! Queen Isabella and King William were there; Queen Eve, Nanny Belle, Prince Ivan and Emilie, Prince Davey and Rosetta and of course the *servants*! Gabriel had left for France at *first light*!

Eve had got the brothers; Donald and Daniel to help her gather the *ashes* of King Roy during the early morning for it looked as if the *snow* was soon to return with the big dark clouds coming their way! King Roy wanted his 'ashes spread' along *the coast of Scotland*; along with - a very SPECIAL REQUEST!

He wanted Eve to *go back* to Prince Edward Island and spread some of his 'ashes' *in their HERB garden* on Prince Edward Island and *along* the *red sandy shore* where they used to live! He knew that she would *have to go back* to let everyone know and to gather whatever *treasures* she had left there when they had came through the Faery Realm with Gabriel; *in such a hurry*!

Their HOME on Prince Edward Island could be a HAVEN for any of *their FAERY FAITH friends* who chose to stay as Peoplefolk and if Tom, Martha or

Sara *wanted to stay* in the wee' Faery Castle or if they chose to be *PEOPLEFOLK size*; they could live in their *big house* by the water! They would be *most welcome*!

Everyone around the table that morning was *surprised* and Eve was *delighted* because she would *love* for 'any of them' *to go with her*! Perhaps she could visit just 'one last time' and do the things King Roy had asked - on the *HEALING shores*; that *she loved so much*! She knew where she had to live now and it was back in Scotland; *with her Daughter*!

"Oh Mother, when would we go?" asked Isabella with *excitement* and *joy* rising up within her. "William would that be possible?" she asked; looking to her King.

Her Mother answered first, "Well Isabella – anyone who would like to go through the *FAERY REALM* would have to go before the 7th day is up at midnight; *if* they have *chosen to stay as PEOPLEFOLK*! And *we could go*; whenever we liked!" Queen Eve said.

William waited for her *response* and then said, "Anytime you like my Queen but perhaps you would need to be back by the 7ᵗʰ day to set up your KINGDOM and re-establish your *rules* of the land! There will be lots to do upon your return!" William added.

"What do you think Emilie? Would you like to go? Perhaps Gabriel and Cecile would *also come*; when they return from France?" Isabella asked excitedly.

"Prince Ivan and I will have to go back to France *as soon as possible* to close up our home and affairs in France Isabella; then return to Scotland and *your Castle Heatheren!*" Emilie answered. "We are to *set sail* on the morrow!"

Prince Ivan said, "I am sure Gabriel would be honored to go with you and take *his beautiful Cecile* to show her the shores of Prince Edward Island and be a part of the 'spreading of the ashes' ceremony!" he added with *warmth* in his voice. Then he looked to his Brother and smiled and said, "I think my Brother and his 'wife to be' will be staying in *Scotland* as he has much to do with becoming the new *THE KING!*"

Again all you could here was the murmurs of, "Hear! Hear!" *in unison* around the kitchen table!

It was Nanny Belles turn to speak up! "My darling Isabella and Eve – I would love to *join you* on your shores of Prince Edward Island as I have heard so much from *you both* about its HEALING ways!" she added!

"Oh Nanny Belle would you; could you?" cried Queen Isabella!

So many things had changed for them all and they all had so many adjustments to make *coming up* and yet it felt like a CELEBRATION and *a time* for NEW BEGINNINGS!

King William spoke up once again trying to *reign in* his Queen with her *child-like joy*; "My Queen – perhaps if you went on *the 3rd day* and stayed *for a night* and *returned on the 4th day*! I will stay here and prepare our *Castle Heatheren II*! The Healing Faeries have already done *great work* on the restoration of it and it would not take much to finish it inside; to your liking!" he added.

"Oh Mother, *it is SETTLED THEN*!" cried Queen Isabella as she jumped up and *hugged* her Mother! She had not felt this *feeling* since she was *16 years old*! She grabbed her Mother and twirled her around; then made Nanny Belle get up and *made her dance around* as well. Rosetta could not sit still; *she too* joined in! They had all joined hands and were going *round* and *round* laughing till the *tears* were coming down their cheeks!

They all laughed and smiled and watched as their beautiful *young* Queen 'let herself go' in *the moment*; 'filling *all their hearts*' with *so much admiration* and pure JOY! She was such an amazing *'child-like woman'* with such a *zest for life* that she made *them feel* a renewed ZEST for life; all of their own! Even the *servants* joined in as they all danced around sharing their child-like *happiness*!

As the *ashes* of her Father sat in the earthen-ware container on the table; everyone was oblivious to the 'purple' *ashes glowing brighter and brighter*; the lid *tap, tap, tapping*; to their glee! Perhaps with this new Covenant with the MAGIC SWORD - 'new ways' of seeing and *communicating* with the Healing Faeries; <u>were already taking shape</u>!

The others knew that *soon enough* they would not be able *to be in the same REALM* so they decided to take

Prince Ivan and Emilie to the ship; the *Alabaster*! They set off in *two* horse drawn carriages; each driven by *six horses*! Queen Isabella rode in the carriage King Rennie had given her when she had arrived back from Prince Edward Island; using *the six white horses* he had *ALSO given her.* King William, Prince Ivan and Emilie rode with them! In the other carriage drawn by *six black horses*; they had Prince Davey, Rosetta, Nanny Belle and Mother Eve and of course *the remains of KING ROY*!

They thought this would be a meaningful time to 'spread his ashes' along the coast of Scotland; just as he *requested*! The *black coach* Queen Eve was in was very fitting for a 'burial ceremony'! The other coach was a fancier one decorated with black and *emerald green* with white scroll etchings on it! They made a *handsome* traveling team as they headed to the coast; *at full speed*!

It was such a jubilant time for what started out to be such a devastating time over the past few months! It was as if TIME had just STOOD STILL for them and finally just 'left them' all to *BE* SPONTANEOUS and <u>FREE</u>! It seemed like now there were no RULES to follow and no matters *pressing them on...*RIGHT NOW <u>they were</u> FREE!

When they arrived at the dock everyone was still excited! They just had enough time left to do a *small ceremony* along the rugged coast; where there coaches sat! They all got out and to their amazement instead of *SNOW*; the clouds had moved *on* and *the sun had come out* while they were riding towards the coastline!

It shone down upon the old sturdy ship and gave it a look of *regal beauty* that it might have had; in years past! The only noise besides the *gentle* stir of the *wind* was the jovial orders the old sea Captain gave - as some people got off the ship! Other carriages had come and were waiting down below, closer to the dock!

It was still cool as the wind whipped around their coats and cloaks and through their hair but it was a *milder wind* compared to the day before!

Queen Eve had some *Lavender* to *mix* with *the ashes* and as she started to let them go from her hand; the *winds came up* and blew them; *all towards her!*

Instead of being *upset* she let out a 'howl of laughter' seeing the *humor side of King Roy;* 'to the end' - still being *playful* with her and she said, "Oh my darling KING ROY you *do not* want to leave me!" As she wiped her lips, her hair and her cloak; she almost looked like a *GHOST* - standing there! Her 'little crowd' of *loved ones* surrounding her could not help but *laugh with her*!

Next, she *tried again;* this time taking out the Kings TARTAN SCARF that he used to wear; filling *some ashes in that* she let it BLOW *out* over the cliff and onto the shore! This time it *blew* and *swirled* perfectly over the side! Then she recited an old *Scottish Healing Faery* prayer and *at the end* whispered softly to the wind, "Till we meet again, *my Husband*; till we *meet again*!"

Everyone hugged her and said their *own* 'goodbyes' to King Roy; in their *own way*! And in turn; they said *goodbye* to Prince Ivan and Emilie before they got on the ship! Isabella was the last one to return to the carriage as she stood *overlooking the sea*!

All of a sudden she shivered and felt a *presence* behind her and *all around her*; she heard her *Father's gentle voice* in the 'winds' *blowing past* her, " My *DARLING DAUGHTER* – I will be there to *CELEBRATE your BIRTHDAY!*" he *whispered* to her, "You *will know* that *it is me*! I loveeeeeeeeeeee **THEE!**" the *windy voice* added.

ISABELLA was so *surprised* and *amazed* that she burst into *fresh tears* crying openly; but they were not tears *of sadness*; but pure JOY as she watched the Alabaster head over the horizon - out to sea, *"MY BIRTHDAY!* FATHER...I *forgot* about *my birthday!* – It will be *during the SEVEN days of the Covenant!* I must go *tell the others!*" she thought as she gathered her warm *velvet* cloak around her. She quickly pulled her Scottish tartan *scarf* from her shoulders and used it to *wipe her eyes* as she *ran back* to the carriage!

As it was, William was waiting for her at the carriage door; for he was ready to go bring her back; so they could leave the coast! Once inside he wrapped her with one of the woolen blankets they all were sharing and they headed back to the Castle Heatheren!

Queen Isabella remained quiet on the ride home! She kept the 'knowledge' of her Father's message *quietly* to herself till she got back! She would share it with them at supper and they too would feel the *sheer miracle* of a *Faery day* it had turned out to be! They all had a little nap' on the way back on the *winding, windy road* to the Castle Heatheren!

When they returned they were delighted in the fact that GABRIEL and CECILE had returned while they had been gone and <u>had</u> *more surprises*!

Gabriel had brought not only *SANDY; his dog,* back through the FAERY REALM *but they had brought back Cecile's FATHER; Pierre*! He had decided to leave his Inn, 'Le Parrot' to his Brother and *come to Scotland* to be with his *only Daughter*! He would remain in the Faery Realm and <u>*not*</u> *in the Peoplefolk Realm;* as he *had been*!

It was a very *refreshing* surprise for all of them. Especially since he had *known* Isabella's *Father* and *Mother*! When Gabriel and Isabella had gone to France; King Roy had sent word to Pierre that Isabella and Gabriel would be arriving and to watch out for them! *Now,* he got to *reunite* with *Queen Eve* and talk about *old times*! What a *small world;* in the world of the FAERY REALM!

During supper Isabella did *share her story* about her Father whispering to her 'through the wind'; *reminding her* about her BIRTHDAY and they all *rejoiced* in the fact that her Father, King Roy was still with them in FAERY SPIRIT and he was guiding them through with his *powerful Faery presence*!

Later that evening after they discussed what everyone was 'doing' over the *next week* they got to relax while *lovely Cecile* played her *harp* for them! She had brought it with her through the Faery Realm; along with some special *French wine* of which they all; *partook*!

Queen Isabella was feeling *much better* and was feeling more *cheerful* for they were leaving the *next morning* to go to her *Fathers' home* on Prince Edward Island!

Prince Davey and his men were going to go back to the Castle Rockland and try to gather his servants together and repair any damage the Mandolins had done and to restore it to its 'proper glory' that it had been! It was also time to bring back the *valuables* and *redecorate* it for his *new bride* and to prepare it for his *big day* when he takes *over the throne* and *becomes KING*! He also had to realign his army and regroup after all that had happened; making sure his Kingdom was *safe* and *secure*! Not to mention the 'reigning in' of King Rennie's *sister* and her husband; they too had to be dealt with for their role in befriending the Captain of the Mandolins!

King William also had to do the same. He and his Queen were to move into their wee' Faery Castle Heatheren II and he had lots to do to make sure the finishing touches were done; *while she was gone.*

It was good' that Queen Isabella was going on this *journey*; it would do her good and when she came back she would feel more in control! With Nanny Belle and her Mother's help they would *align* with the Healing Faeries to bring *back* the Healing Remedies they had put away for *safe keeping* in their *special* Faery 'hiding places'! They needed to *get organized* so they could help *both* the *Faeryfolk* and *Peoplefolk* alike; who were *in* need of their <u>HEALING WAYS</u>!

At first light Prince Davey and Rosetta stood watching as the TRAVELING PARTY was getting *ready* to leave for the Island! Pierre, Cecile's Father had left early to go to the Castle Heatheren II; he had been a handyman and had *worked with stone* (before he ran the Inn) so he wanted to be a part of the team *restoring* the Castle!

They all gathered in the courtyard all dressed in their winter cloaks; scarves and hats! There was a variety of satchels, instruments and even Sandy; Gabriel's dog was going back to Prince Edward Island for this *MEMORABLE* trip! Donald, Daniel and William helped them rearrange their things they were taking with them! Mother Eve had her husband's urn with her; Cecile her harp, Gabriel his dog and Queen Isabella had some of their Healing Faerie wine and some French wines with her in leather flasks to take for gifts'!

William watched as they said their 'Healing Faery chant' they used to help them *enter* into the *Faery Realm*. He felt a 'tug at his heart' as he watched his brave Isabella and her Mother make this journey -*for her Father*! He almost wished he too could just leave everything behind for a couple of days and just go – but he felt a responsibility towards all those who were coming to their Castle to see what the *future holds*; he had to be there for *his people*!

It was the same for Prince Davey who had to return to the Castle Rockland later that day; it was time to show his Kingdom *a new way of life!* He had to RESTORE a KINGDOM; not *just a Castle!*

William felt that *strange rush* – as they all *disappeared;* before him! He didn't feel like being *alone* so he asked the two Brothers, the Prince and Rosetta to come in for some hot broth and tea *by the fire!*

"Come inside Brothers for some tea and broth – you are most welcome to *sit with us* before the Prince has to *leave!*" William said. "Aye, we still have so much to talk about; let us do it by the fire! It has been a busy *last two days!*" Prince Davey added. Donald and Daniel agreed and followed them to the main entrance.

When they went inside Rosetta; used to being a servant herself, helped the kitchen staff *prepare* their table! Prince Davey *smiled to himself!* He was *looking forward* to his life with Rosetta!

When the 'five happy Healing Faeries' arrived on the shores of Prince Edward Island they were not prepared; for <u>*all the SNOW*</u>! It must have snowed for days for there was barely a path to Queen Eve's *front door*! Luckily the *sun* was shining when they arrived and it was still early enough for them to have 'lots of hours' of *daylight left* to do the things they planned! The dog barked and frolicked around in the snow which caused Tom and Martha to come out from their small wee' Faery Castle to *investigate* what all the fuss was about!

Martha was the *first* to start *yelling* and *laughing* all at the same time when she saw *Sandy*; the dog! She flew *back and forth* in the wee' Faery Realm and told Tom they better become the size of Peoplefolk *fast*; before the *dog* gets them!

"Tom! Tom!" she cried. "We have guests – *go get Sara*; its ISABELLA, EVE and *Gabriel*!" she added as she quickly became *Peoplefolk size*, in the 'blink of an eye'! She then ran wildly *through the snow* to see them! She was a bit older than Nanny Belle and Eve but she had the energy of the 'tireless youth'; *in their prime*! She was a joy to behold for the *five Healing Faeries* standing before her!

In a flurry of 'hugs and kisses' she made her rounds and was so glad to meet Nanny Belle whom she had *heard so much about* and to meet *beautiful Cecile*! Quickly, Tom and Sara joined them!

"Come, Come!" Tom said. "You are welcome to come to either home' – we have the 'home fires' burning in *both*!" he added in a jovial manner. Tom was always such a host!

"Let us go to *our home* Tom!" Queen Eve said delightedly! "You sure have had lots of *snow* on the Island!" she added. "Follow us everyone, let's *lighten* our load!" she said cheerfully following Tom on the small path towards the house and the veranda! Everyone was talking at once and it was like you could feel 'your burdens roll' off your shoulders already, in just the *few minutes* of being on the *healing SHORES* of *Prince Edward Island*!

Once inside Martha ushered them into the kitchen by the hearth and fire! Everyone sat down their packages and satchels! The dog already took *his place* lying on the woolen mat by the fire! They took off their cloaks and winter attire and gathered around the table! Martha made them some *tea* and brought out some biscuits! She always knew what they needed! This gave Queen Eve a chance to tell them about *KING ROY* which set *some tears to fall*; for they had *wondered* why *he was NOT with them*; not *a part* of the *HOME COMING*!

Queen Eve begged to differ, "Oh but Martha, Tom and Sara; dear *King Roy* is *with us*!" as she used her finger to tap on the URN she had sat on the *side table*! She watched as their mouths dropped with *oh's* and *ah's* as they figured out; just what was inside the earthen-ware container!

Queen Isabella was the one *to share* what had taken place and about the COVENANT! She thought they may as well know *right away* for they only were staying for a 'short time' before they had to leave to go back to Scotland! She wanted them to spread the word through the FAERY REALM on Prince Edward Island so they all would have a CHOICE of where they would like to be!

The three of them *were shocked* at all the *news* that their Queen had just given them! They too found some chairs to sit down and Isabella and Nanny Belle thought they should *perhaps* light some *Frankincense* and *some Lavender oil* for them! The three of them had some choices to make in a matter of days; before the COVENANT was up!

Queen Isabella was glad that her Mother and Nanny Belle were there to *assist her* in sharing their thoughts and *sharing* what they had planned to do!

Queen Eve went on the say, "It was my husband's *request* to leave some of his ashes' along the shore; to mix 'with the red Island soil' *and* to leave some in *our Herb garden!*" she added with a smile on her face. "Do you think we could take *this time* while the *sun is still shining* to spread *King Roy's ashes* in the garden where the Hollyhocks and the climbing Roses go?" she asked. "We have such little time' to be with you!"

"Of course, Love!" said Martha. "Tom, Sara; let us get ready – let us make a path for them!" she added. Martha was really a *sweetheart* and knew when to 'do and say' the *right things*!

"*We* shall help you!" said Gabriel and Cecile.

"While you are doing that I will get Nanny Belle and Isabella to help me rummage through some of King Roy's special things'/treasures to see if there is anything I need of his; to *go* with the ashes'!" Queen Eve said.

"Mother!" said Isabella. "I have an idea!" she answered. "Let us get a *small box* – do you have any 'special boxes' that we can put a few things in for Father to *leave in* the garden *with him*?" she asked.

"Well yes, I do Lass! Good idea!" her Mother answered back. "Come with me!" she said as she nodded for Nanny Belle to follow them too.

Her Mother found a *velvet box* she had with her blue-green crystal barrette in it and she started with that! Then she found some Lavender to sprinkle into it – and a Scottish *pin* she had with *their Clan's crest* on it!

"Oh Eve – that is lovely *so far!*" said Nanny Belle.

"Oh, MOTHER do you still have those BLUE JAY feathers Father found one day by the shore?" Isabella asked starting to get more *excited* for this part of the ceremony!

"Yes! They are lying on the hearth in the kitchen Isabella; on the small *stone* shelves; on the *left hand side of the fireplace*; if you can reach them!" she added.

Isabella went to get the feathers' and met them coming back through the kitchen with some 'other small items' they had found! Eve had found some *buttons* off his cloak with the Scottish Thistle *etched* in them – knowing he would *love* that gesture! Together they put them inside and covered the box over with a *small piece* of their Clan tartan and tied it with some *leather* ties!

"Let's go meet the others!" Mother Eve said as she quickly got on her *cloak* and *scarf.* "Isabella could you grab your Fathers walking stick by the door he loved so much; the one with the *Thistle* carved in the top of the handle?" she asked as she went to pick up the Urn on the table!

"I will get the door!" said Nanny Belle.

Together they met the others in the garden by the wall of the house! There were still some branches and stems of the Hollyhocks and the wild *climbing* Rose bush going up the side of the house; brown now by the fall and winter season; but still showing... They were *HIS FAVOURITES*! There was *no wind* which was odd for the Island – there usually was a breeze blowing; especially with the snow – but for some reason; all was *CALM*! She smiled to herself as she remembered what had happened that day they were standing along the coast in Scotland; when the wind' came back - blowing the *KING'S ashes*; into *her face*!

Gabriel and Tom knocked back the snow from the bushes using their hands and King Roy's *walking stick*! They had gotten right down to the ground so they could easily leave the VELVET BOX hidden beneath the *Rose bush*, near the earth; then using the stick - they enclosed the snow all around it!

Then; Eve began to speak, "We are gathered here today my HUSBAND for your *last wishes*! YOU are among *your faithful* loyal Faery Friends and your adoring Wife and Daughter and the *SON* you never had!" she added as she looked up at Gabriel's dark blue eyes staring back at her. "We shall *never forget you*; you will be in *our HEARTS forever'* and may you *live on through us* - for the rest of *our days*! Till we *meet again*!" she added gracefully! Eve gently *spread his ashes* over the trail of Hollyhocks and Rose bushes; then in turn gave some to *everyone* to help *spread* his ashes throughout their garden! It was fitting for King Roy's ashes to 'linger there' for he had *loved* and *treasured* his 'herb and flower' garden so much and had spent many hours *lovingly taking care of it*! You could *smell* the Lavender in the cool air as they *mixed it in* and it was most *welcoming* and *becoming* for their Clan and *very healing*!

After they were done there, they all walked down the hill carefully; towards the *shoreline*! The closer you got to the water the more you could see the 'red soil' standing out *against* the pure *white snow*! Once again they all 'spread his ashes' out into the Ocean! Along the shore you could start to feel *the wind* coming up from the North and you could see the *dark clouds* coming up over the horizon!

Queen Eve, Nanny Belle, Tom and Martha headed back up the rocky shore leaving the younger ones *to linger*!

"Remember Gabriel the day I arrived on the shores of Prince Edward Island?" Isabella asked. "Almost on this very spot!" she added.

"Aye, I do!" answered Gabriel. It was almost as if Sandy his dog sensed it too; for she started barking and barking at them all as they stood along the shore! She sniffed at the ashes and the Lavender on the ground and then bounded *up the trail* to the house for *she knew the way HOME*; for she had lived there before, too!

"Let's go back up now!" said Isabella. They both followed her up as she talked about her love of Prince Edward Island and their time there together!

Cecile loved the Island – even though it was not summer or spring she could *sense* how beautiful it was and she loved the *red soil*! She had never seen soil that *color* before and she thought she may have to come back with Gabriel another time when she could run through that *red sand* with her *bare feet*! She shivered now at the thought of it! She hurried trying to keep up with Isabella, Gabriel and *his dog*!

When they got back up to the house – the others had a surprise for Isabella since she was to CELEBRATE *her birthday* on the Island! Tom was going to go over to their neighbors to borrow their *sleigh* so they could take her for a sleigh ride for they knew how much she had loved it; *on her 16th birthday*!

Once Martha knew there was to be a CELEBRATION she soon got extra help from some of the other Healing Faeries to help *step up* the festivities! It was also a time for Isabella and her Mother and the others to share the news about the COVENANT; in person, from the *Royal family*!

Nanny Belle and Cecile went into the woods and collected some PINE boughs to decorate the hearth, the veranda and the sleigh! Pine was one of the Healing Faeries favorite healing tools they used!

The *oil of Pine* was used to invigorate your spirits and *refresh your soul*! It was also used for colds and flu and if used in small doses; in candle wax for burning! But tonight it was not only gathered for the

CELEBRATION of Isabella's coming birthday - but to CELEBRATE *the Winter Solstice!*

The winter was a very special time for the Healing Faeries - it felt like Christmas and Birthdays all *rolled into one!* Oh they had their *own Christmas time* in the Faery Realm! Not like our Christmas of *today* but it was the time of the Winter Solstice – the time for *purification and light!* The winter and the snow made people REFLECT and take *more time* to be *cozy* – a time for *slowing down* the pace of life! Seeing the snow falling softly covering everything in nature's pure white; was *healing* for people! And then there were the *snow angels;* which really WERE *snow angels;* in the Faery Realm!

This time they decided to go for their ride just before dark and they were going to try to go along the shoreline this time or as close to it as they could! There was supposed to be a *full moon* that night so coming onto dusk; if luck would have it; they may see the Moon filtering through *the oncoming clouds!*

There was *merriment* around her Father's house that night! The news had spread that her family was home and soon there was a crowd waiting to see them off!

Ned, the owner of the sleigh, had come; to *be their driver*! All warm and cozy in their sleigh; with heavy woolen blankets and bricks from the fire for their feet; they headed off *towards the shoreline*!

This time there was just Gabriel and Cecile, Nanny Belle, Mother Eve and Isabella! The others stayed back at the house preparing the food and getting the *wine and spirits'* ready for their return!

The air was crisp and there was just a small breeze when they headed out! You could hear the *jingle* of the sleigh bells on the horses harness and on the *sides* of the sleigh! You could hear the waves of the Ocean at times when they were able to get close to it! And the beautiful Moon *did appear* over the Ocean and Isabella made everyone make a WISH even though they were celebrating; *her birthday*! They giggled and laughed when Queen Isabella pulled out a *flask* of the Healing Faery *wine* for them all to share on the way back! She was certainly 'one of a kind' our Royal Highness! Her Mother had brought 'more of her Father's ashes' with her and sprinkled them here and there on their sleigh ride; she thought for *sure* King Roy would like that! Although she did say on the way back she would keep the '*rest of KING ROY for herself*' to *take back with her* to Scotland!

Once again the mood turned *festive* and the *gentle* Healing Faery folk were able to *feel that FREEDOM they so desired and were able to just be <u>themselves</u>!*

When they arrived back in the yard their *joyful rosy faces* were aglow and the *full moon* was out in full force shining down upon the crowd that had gathered waiting for them on the veranda and surrounding the house! Tom and Gabriel had made a bonfire out in front of the house for people to stay warm and drinks and food were already being handed out!

Gathering around the bonfire Queen Isabella talked to the crowd about the *Covenant* and what it meant for each of them! She told them all about what *had happened* in Scotland when they had to use the *Invisible Realm* to fight against the Mandolins! She also shared with them what had happened to *her Father*, King Roy and how she wanted them to know how much they all had meant to him; *all these years!*

Queen Eve also spoke to the crowd *thanking them* for their love and kindness which had surrounded them on the 'healing shores' of their Island all these years and that she would be staying in Scotland with *her daughter*; the *Queen of the Healing Faeries*! She ended with telling them *this*, " I want you all to use our HOME as a *haven* for those who choose to remain as Peoplefolk and our wee' small Castle on the shoreline of Howards Cove for the wee' folk to visit and to stay close with one another! Even though we are entering into a *new way* of RULING *LIKE THE WIND* – we have to remain *united* and *not drift apart*! Now more than ever we have to stand by each other's side and support one another <u>as the true Patriot Healing Faeries *that we are*</u>!" she added with strength and *conviction* in her voice!

The crowd applauded and cheered with *small murmurs* of, "Hear, Hear!" (These words were *common*ly used among the Healing Faeries! When you *agreed* with what someone *was saying* you would answer; "Hear, Hear!")

Tom spoke up next and said, "Let the festivities begin! We are graced with lovely Cecile heralding from France playing her *beautiful harp* and of course

from France playing her *beautiful harp* and of course you all know Gabriel who will play his *tin whistle!"* he added in his cheerful voice, "When you get cold you are *welcome inside* the wee' Castle or inside King Roy and Queen Eve's HOME! There is plenty of refreshments and *food for all!"*

There were just as many *well wishers* as there were people talking to Eve about the *loss* of her husband! And just as many *Happy Birthday wishes* for Queen Isabella *and many gifts' – small momentums,* for her to take with her!

Nanny Belle was having so much *fun* talking with everyone! She loved the Islanders and felt very much at home there! She loved Martha, Tom and Sara. Isabella was happy to hear Tom and Martha had gotten together as a couple and they had already decided to STAY in the Peoplefolk Realm (which really *surprised her)* and that they would like to be the 'caretakers' of *her Mother's home* on Prince Edward Island! Sara wanted to stay in the Faery Realm and had asked if she could be the *caretaker* of the *wee' Castle!*

There was much talk among all the Healing Faeries that had come to join in the festivities and with this sudden *news* of the Covenant; it seemed *many of them* had made their choices, *that night*!

Queen Isabella looked radiant that night in her blue velvet cloak – the color blue, *matching her eyes*! Although she was *happy* she was not feeling very good so she took Nanny Belle aside to tell her!

"Nanny Belle could you come into the house with me for a moment?" she asked. Nanny Belle had just been dancing on the veranda with 'a handsome Islander'; one of the Healing Clan folk who owned the SLEIGH they had been on! She grabbed onto Isabella's arm and escorted her inside!

"Isabella what is wrong?" she asked. "You have a worried look on your face *Darling*!" she said.

"I am feeling *ill* Nanny Belle!" she answered. "I hope it is not something *I ate*!" she added. "I feel a bit dizzy and I have not even had one dance yet!" she said trying to *make light* of it!

"Oh, Issy – come upstairs where *it is quieter*! There are so many people here this evening! I have not had this much *fun* in years!" she laughed as she guided

Isabella into one of the bedrooms. "Come child and lay down a spell – let us get your cloak off! You must be exhausted with everything you have gone through!" she added.

"Oh Nanny Belle you better get me a wet cloth for my head and maybe some healing remedies; my Crystal stones; *something*!" she said as she lay down, on the bed!

"Alright... Isabella!" Nanny Belle answered starting to get concerned for her! She went back down to the main area of the house to find Isabella's leather pouch; she *usually* kept by her side. When she found it she went out on the veranda to look for Queen Eve. She found her inside in the kitchen cutting up some bread for the big 'pot of soup' they had - *stewing over the fire*!

"Eve!" Nanny Belle said. "Could you come with me for a moment to see Isabella; she is not feeling well!" she added softly.

"Of course!" answered Queen Eve. Sara took over for her while she went with Nanny Belle. When they got back up to the room Isabella had already been up and had been sick.

"Oh dear!" said her Mother. "How long have you been feeling ill Isabella?" she asked.

"Well I was not feeling good when we entered the Faery Realm early this morning Mother! I have eaten today and only had the *one drink* of wine/spirits on *our sleigh ride*!" she answered.

"Come here Isabella!" her Mother said as she lit more candles around the room! Isabella went to her Mother and she felt her head. She did not seem warm! "Let me look at you!"

Nanny Belle looked at Eve and was trying NOT to think of thoughts of poison or any possibility of someone hurting Isabella! She held her thoughts for now!

"Come – lay down Isabella!" her Mother said. "I will get *a blanket* to put over you and get Gabriel to make a fire in this room to keep it warm!" she added.

"I will go to get him Eve!" said Nanny Belle and I will bring up some *special* tea and I will make it *myself!*" she added with assurance!

"Very well!" answered Eve.

She then went over to sit by her Daughter on the bed! "Isabella you have just gone through a lot – no wonder you are not feeling well – *my Child!*" she said soothingly. "Let me get your healing Crystal stones out for you *to hold.* Nanny Belle is bringing you some *hot tea* as well!" she added.

"Okay Mother!" Isabella said faintly as she *closed her eyes.* Eve looked around the familiar room; taking in the herbs that were hanging over the windows, the comfy homemade furniture she loved. While she was looking around the room she looked up on the hooks that lined one side of wall which had some cloaks and some odds and ends of clothes hanging on them! She spotted an apron of Isabella's she had kept from when Isabella was just twelve years old! It was the first one Isabella had sewn on her own; with Nanny Belle's help! It was dusty and getting old but she smiled at the memories of Isabella as a small wee' Faery child and how she *loved* getting into *so much mischief!*

Before long Nanny Belle had come back with tea and as they both turned to look at Isabella; she was *fast asleep*! They both smiled up at one another and Nanny Belle sat the tea by her bedside!

"Let us go down and perhaps we can start saying *our goodbyes* and *our goodnights* and things will *settle* for the evening!" said Queen Eve as Nanny Belle knowingly smiled at her! "It sure has been a *whirlwind of a day* for us all!"

Within the hour the Homestead of King Roy and Queen Eve was all *quiet* once again! Some of the Healing Faeries had stayed and helped Martha and Sara tidy up and Tom and Gabriel had made sure the fires were out outside and things tidied up out there! *King Roy* was *safely* put back up on the 'side table' in the kitchen and Sandy lay snoring on the kitchen floor by the hearth! Queen Eve went up to check on Isabella and she was still sleeping; so that was good! She needed a good night's sleep and *hopefully* she would feel better in the morning!

A peaceful quietness had crept into the Homestead and you could just hear the faint noise *of the wood* in the fireplaces hissing and sizzling as the large logs burned through the night keeping them all warm and cozy. Queen Eve had slipped into the other side of Isabella's big bed so she could watch over her through the night; in case she still felt ill. But even more so perhaps to *quiet* the *loneliness* and the *void* she felt *already* without her devoted husband; King Roy by her side! She would *miss him* - till the *end of her days*!

They woke to the sound of Sandy barking when Martha and Sara had come in the early morning to *stoke the fires* for them! Isabella stirred when she had heard the dog and as soon as she sat up; she instantly, felt *ill at ease;* again. Her Mother sat up with her and said, "Oh my goodness ISABELLA – I think I know what is wrong!" she said with a surprised - shocked expression on her face!

Isabella sleepily turned around and looked at her Mother strangely. "I think you are *with CHILD!*" she announced right out of the blue!

"What, MOTHER?" she asked in a surprised voice filled with awe.

"You were fine through the night and now at first light you are *ill* again!" her Mother answered with *a knowing smile.*

"Oh my goodness!" said Isabella. "How can you tell?" she asked.

"Are your clothes getting *tighter* around your belly, Issy?" her Mother asked as she looked for the truth on her Daughter's face.

"Well come to think of it – my *velvet cloak* felt uncomfortable on me yesterday!" Isabella said putting her hands on her belly.

Just then Isabella started to sit up on the side of the bed and saw something lying on her pillow. She picked up a 'piece of clothing' and as she did so; something *small* rolled onto the floor! Isabella held up her 'small apron' as she *gently* bent over and picked up a *button*! A button from her FATHERS CLOAK! One of the buttons, with the Scottish Thistle etched on it! Isabella held them both up to show her MOTHER and as she did; a *SECOND button* fell to the floor!

"Mother; it's my *old apron* and TWO buttons off *of Father's cloak!*" Isabella cried. Her Mother got up and came over to Isabella and stood her up and hugged her!

"Your Father; has once again left a sign' for us! You are with CHILD and *perhaps TWINS!*" her Mother answered! It was very rare for a woman to have *TWINS* within the Faery Realm but perhaps once again it was Isabella's destiny to be; *THE ONE!*

"Oh Mother maybe that is why I am so weepy these days – I have heard that a pregnant woman can cry more often when she is with CHILD!" she answered as she started to tear up at just the thought of it all! Her Mother just held her and just felt another MIRACLE had just happened – *here on Prince Edward Island!* Here it was; this close to Isabella's birthday and her dear Father was still leaving them *signs!*

Eve held the 'small apron' in her arms and the *buttons* in her hand and it was all too much; she *had to have - her own cry!* It was Isabella's turn to go to her MOTHER and let her shed her own tears of 'happiness and sorrow'; all at the *same time!*

To *feel* the love of the Healing Faeries and to actually see the *meaningful miracles* that surrounded them every day was one of life's; *true blessings*!

Mother and Daughter got themselves together and got dressed to go down and see the others! This was there last day on the Island and they had *much to accomplish*!

The kitchen was a warm welcome for them and the others were *cheerfully* up and *ready* for their day! Nanny Belle and Martha had prepared breakfast and Sara had stoked all the fireplaces and had everything *cozy* for them! They all were ready to help in any way they could with Eve's *packing*!

Cecile and Gabriel were already out in the barn visiting the horses! It was snowing softly and to look out; there were no *telltale signs* that there had been *a crowd* out there the night before or a sleigh ride; with horses!

Ned, the man who owned the sleigh came by and stayed for a cup of tea with them that morning! He seemed much taken with Nanny Belle and you could tell he listened to 'every word' she said and *perhaps she felt the same;* for Isabella noticed she had not seen her *blush* so much as she *had - that morning*! So many things were *happening so fast* - it was hard for Isabella to keep up with it all!

After he left; she went around the 'old homestead' and helped her Mother pick out a *few special things* she wanted to take back with her! They would all help her carry things and all *the larger things*; would *remain intact*! Eve wanted to keep the place relatively the same in case they ever wanted to come back to visit or perhaps with Isabella with child – bring *her children* there someday!

They also had the *wee' Faery Castle* to stay in should they ever return and Sara *promised* she would take *good care of it for them*!

With their 'extraordinary powers' they could make things get *smaller* or *larger* but now it would only be *those who chose to stay in* the Faery Realm who would be able to do that! EVERYTHING was about to *change*; for *all* of them!

When they had everything packed they decided to enjoy the rest of the day before they entered into the Faery Realm to return to Scotland! Queen Eve had a special request for Cecile and Gabriel; she wanted them to play the *Healing Faeries song* for them as they gathered around the fire' in the main room of the house! Cecile played her small harp and Gabriel accompanied her with his tin whistle! Tom also joined in with them for he had taught Gabriel to play; just years before! It was a special time for them and a *meaningful one*; in *three* more days all their lives would be changed *forever*!

Just before they were *leaving,* an incredible thing happened! Ned their 'Healing Faery neighbor' came up to the Homestead in his sleigh; *his horses* prancing and dancing; their *sleigh bells* ringing *and* Ned with his satchel; *on his back*! He offered the horses and the sleigh for Tom and Martha if they chose to take them and he *openly* asked Nanny Belle if she minded if he accompanied her *back to Scotland*! He was born there and had come to the Island to be with his only Brother who had moved there! He told them he worked with stone and he was sure there was 'plenty of work to be done' with many Faery Homes to be built within the Faery Realm and he *was READY*!

Tom and Martha told them they would love to be the *proud owners* of his sleigh and horses and would take good care of them for him! Then *everyone* watched Nanny Belle; *waiting* to hear *her REPLY*!

With their lives changing so fast and being in the moment Nanny Belle replied, "Well Ned – I think we could always use another *good worker* in the Faery Realm and if you *did not like it* you could *always return!*" she answered her face turning as red; *as her hair*! Gabriel spoke up for Nanny Belle and replied, "We could always use a good Patriot of the Healing Faeries; especially now and we have heard many good things about you from King Roy! You will be like most of us returning; choosing *to live* in the Wee' Faery Realm'! Welcome *aboard!*" he added as he shook his hand.

Queen Eve was so proud of Gabriel at that moment! What a fine gentleman he had *turned out* to be! This ISLAND and its *healing – shores* were truly - *good for the SOUL!*

Mother and Daughter were now *ready* to return to Scotland! They had fulfilled their duty to her Father and they all had *prospered* from their visit! Tom and Martha now stood on the threshold of their new PEOPLEFOLK lives and were now the *official owners* and *caretakers* of the *Howards Cove Homestead*! It was time to go HOME!

Now, there were *six* Healing Faeries standing with arms 'full of treasures' - <u>ready</u> to *enter into the Faery Realm*!

When *they arrived* in Scotland; they *reappeared* in the courtyard of the Castle Heatheren! Nanny Belle had put her arm through Ned's - to guide him through to their destination; Gabriel had held Sandy, his dog and *everyone else* had their *arms full of treasures*!

They were glad to have made it and when they arrived it was snowing *heavily*; *almost like a blizzard*! No *sunshine* for their arrival back in Scotland; it was *bleak* and *cold*! Winter was settling in all around them; *wherever* they travelled! Wallace ran out from the stables barking; welcoming *them* HOME! Donald and Daniel followed him and saw that the *small group* had returned from the Island and ran to *help them* carry in their things! They all *hurried* into the Castle Heatheren; escaping the snow and the cold!

Lenora, the main house keeper met them at the door and told them William was in the main Library if they wanted to go in where it was *warm*!

The other maids and staff scurried about for the Queen and her Mother making sure 'all was well' for them! William was *so happy* to see them! He almost lifted Isabella right off the floor to hold her; he had missed *her so*!

Nanny Belle introduced her son, King William to her new friend and *fellow Healing Faery*; Ned who had accompanied them back from Prince Edward Island! He *shook hands* with the King and took a bow *before him*! Ned told him he had been thinking of coming back home to Scotland and now that he knew about the *Covenant* he wanted to come back and do *whatever he could* to help rebuild and restore the Healing Faeries *Homes, Castles and Havens*!

Once they all got *settled in* and *comfy* William told them that Roland had came back from France through the Faery Realm and had visited with Prince Ivan, Emilie and *Queen Ivy*!

"Right now he is over helping Pierre, Cecile's Father; they're both at the Castle Heatheren II making sure it gets finished for us by the *seventh day*!" he added.

"How was *my Mother* - did he say when they are returning?" asked Gabriel anxious to hear how they were doing!

"He said they looked *wonderful*; considering all they had been through and that they wanted to *come back* as soon as possible on the *very next ship*!" William answered. They all were in *good spirits* and they loved to spend time together; it was such a blessing *NOW* that *they had the FREEDOM*; *to do so*! They all sat around for awhile longer and took their leisurely time to have tea and *shared more* about what had *happened* during their journey to Prince Edward Island!

Before long *Pierre and Roland* came back and *joined in* and Queen Isabella announced that they should all go freshen up and prepare to have supper together *later* that evening!

The <u>Castle Heatheren</u> was *once again* 'filled with good cheer' and those that knew King William and Isabella;

also knew about their *outstanding hospitality*! Everyone had pitched in and helped *them* replace their sturdy homemade furniture, decorations and treasures' that they had *hidden* during the *Mandolin's raids*! Their castle had always been *known* for its *soothing* and *comfy atmosphere* and with its *unique design*; was a HAVEN not only for the *wee' Faeryfolk* but for the *Peoplefolk size* as well and *would remain that way* for the rest of their days!

Finally; when *Queen Isabella* had King William <u>all to herself</u> she could not hold back the *news* about the *possibility* she was with *child* and *perhaps even TWINS*! Isabella was excited to finally be able to share this news with her husband; *her KING*! He was shocked and elated about the news and felt such great happiness; he stood there *staring at her*; searching for *telltale signs*!

"Oh Isabella, my BEAUTIFUL QUEEN – *YOUR WITH CHILD*!" he exclaimed lovingly! "Are you alright? How do *you feel about it all*?" William asked excitedly; *searching* her *beautiful face* for answers.

"I feel blessed William – *TRULY BLESSED*!" she answered. "At first I was feeling a wee' bit queasy in the mornings but now I feel fine!" she added cheerfully. "But soon Husband I will be as *big* as *this CASTLE;* if I am *with TWINS!*" she added as she *ran into his arms...* "Will you still *love me – then,* William?" Isabella asked as she smiled up at him.

"I will love you *more* my Queen – I will *LOVE YOU MORE!*" he said as he kissed her! "And by the way; you will be *smaller* in the wee' FAERY REALM my Isabella and you will not *notice it as much!*" he laughed; *teasing with her!* "Come, *rest with me!*" he added.

Isabella laughed with him; to think of them *together,* in the *wee'* Faery Realm! She had seen William *mostly* in the *Peoplefolk Realm* and as *Peoplefolk size;* it will be different for her to see him there!

"I am so *happy for us* Isabella – to think things have turned out so well *in the midst of such CHAO'S;* such upheaval!" he added. "We are so *blessed* and now *FREE* to live our *lives to the fullest!* Everyone is choosing *their own path* and in *those choices* I see *peace* and *happiness* and *new beginnings* 'My Queen'!" he said thoughtfully.

"You are right; My King! Even *my* Mother and *your* *Mother* will be with us and we will have *wee'* FAERY CHILDREN; *of our own...*" she added; starting to get *teary eyed* once again! "I am so *very grateful* and *thankful* for this day – for this chance; for this *new beginning*! May our love carry us through and guide us in our weeks and months and *years to come!*" she added as she touched her belly gently; as William *held her*!

Isabella put her hand in her pouch and took out her *Father's braid* and laid it in her lap – she held the *buttons* from his cloak and looked down at *his ring* upon her finger and she thought about the words of *King Rennie* and *her Father* and said, "I can *Run Like the Wind* or I can *Ride Like the Wind* but the <u>pact</u> is to *Rule Like the Wind*! I shall *BE like the wind*, William! In the Invisible Realm our children will *never* have to *choose* where they want to live – they will live out their days with us and have the *freedom* that I knew when I was a *wee'* Faery Child; embracing those *innocent, magical, moments* in time!" she added holding her Father's braid to her *heart*! "William! *My dream IS coming true* - THE HEALING FAERIES are now FREE to be *whoever they want to be* and to live out their days sharing their gifts' with others! No one will know *where* or *who* they are!" Queen Isabella said. "*We are FREE!*" she shouted triumphantly!

"*Hear! Hear;* my Queen – *Hear; Hear!*" answered King William as he smiled over at his beautiful wife.

As she stood up; she took the arm of *her King* and said, "Let's go down and *join* the others! WE only have *three more days* to be together *in this ONE REALM;* then *on to our NEW BEGINNING!*"

Their friends and family were *overjoyed* to hear the news that Isabella was with child and to the Healing Faeries nothing could be more of a *'new beginning'* than to know they were going to have *two new born children* to carry on the Healing Ways and to start a *new generation* of Healing Faeries!

This was indeed a HAPPY ENDING to the *long road* 'to FREEDOM' for *Isabella* and *the Healing Faeries!* THE END.......

THE MEANING OF THE WORDS:
<u>RULES LIKE THE WIND</u>

****

R - RADIATE

U - Understanding

L - LOVE & LAUGH (often)

E - Experience

S - SPONTANEOUS

L - Laughter & Love

I - INVITE & INVITING

K - Kindness

E - EVERYDAY

T - Thankfulness & Timelessness

H - HAPPINESS & HOPE

E - Earthly and Elemental

W - WORTHINESS

I - Interwoven Invisibly (together)

N - NATURALLY

D - Divine

****

THE FAERY CREED – FOR THE HEALING FAERIES

(From BOOK I to BOOK III; here is the *full HEALING FAERY CREED!*)

Till Heaven above and the Earth we love *are as one* – we will never leave you! The Faeryfolk believe everything you will ever need is in this <u>very moment</u>... EMBRACE it – cherish it and respect it. With each new sunrise you have a chance to *begin again*!

The Healing Faeries also believe we still have time <u>TO HEAL OUR MOTHER EARTH</u>... Each one of us before this day is through...Do something to help save our 'Heaven on Earth' – Walk more, drive less, pick up litter or plant another TREE! We can make a difference for our children – just do it and see...The time is NOW – the place is EARTH – love it to life – *CREATE HER REBIRTH*!

Tis' time to RULE LIKE THE WIND and bring the INVISIBLE to us and just like the WIND use our *invisible forces* to assist with the Healing of the WORLD; ourselves and our environment *we live in*! Tis' time for us to <u>REMEMBER</u> we each have the power to HEAL; <u>IT'S</u> *inside us already*.......

From *within* as *without*
From the *inner* to the *outer*
As *above* as *below*

It is a time to put <u>*all individuality aside*</u> and to BE AS ONE! It is TIME for ACTION; *not REACTION!* Surround yourself *NOW* with *loving, kind, energetic souls!* Hug more, share more <u>unconditional love</u> *with one another!* Here's to the speedy recovery of our Earth and to the LOVE, COURAGE and DEVOTION of each one of us who truly care; men, women, children – the elementals and the *earth itself!*

Help us to RECREATE 'Heaven on Earth' as it was meant to be... THE TIME IS NOW! DO NOT DELAY! TODAY IS THE DAY! TAKE <u>this time</u> to *invest* your POSITIVE ENERGY into every *breath* and *every step you take* – <u>for our *Mother Earth's* sake</u>!

(You are never alone in your journey!
Finally and most importantly: NEVER give up!)

Sprinkles of LOVE and FAERY DUST...
Isabella, *Queen of the Healing Faeries*

EPILOGUE

'To be a Healing Faery at *that time* was a great *'life to live'*...to be able to be both of the *Faery Realm* and of the *Peoplefolk Realm* was <u>indeed</u> a great *place to be*...For *no other time in history;* was *this FREEDOM* to be!'

A quiet eeriness took on the days and weeks following that <u>last day of battle!</u> One thing was certain – *no one* would out due the Healing Faeries EVER AGAIN! The FREEDOM of the Healing Faeries is now a *guarded one*...and again a choice for 'each one' of them *but* from that day forward; on the *day* her FATHER died on the Faery Bridge; on that 7th day of December; the PEOPLEFOLK do not know and <u>will not know</u> where they have *all scattered*!

Within the Faery Realm the Faeries still have *special privileges* and the Healing Faeries who have chosen to stay as Peoplefolk can still see them but their <u>SECRECY</u> is intact and it is *rare indeed* to be in their presence and a *special sighting* is in store for those 'whose *eyes*' can still *see them*!

Isabella was with child and a *possibility* of having TWIN Faery children which was rare *in the Faery Realm*! Her children would be *part* of the Secret Realm but would *never* be part of the 'way it used to be'! *Now* more than ever there was *much work to be done* and once again the Healing Faeries (Clan book) was being rewritten for their *new lives* –within the SECRET Realm! The Healing Faeries were Invisible but <u>not *dispensable*</u>; Invisible but <u>not *destructible*</u>!

Now that they were in their SECRET FAERY REALM; they were <u>safe</u> and *now FREE*!

For those who followed their QUEEN and chose not to be as *Peoplefolk* again – they would remain in the wee' Faery Realm and travel through the Faery Realm *invisibly* doing their HEALING WORK! With the new COVENANT they actually had MORE POWERS! They could transform *large things; to small* and *small things to large*...but they also respected' this right!

Queen Isabella took her horse Gladiator and *their dogs* Samuel and Wallace with them into the wee'

Faery Realm! Anything they had in the PEOPLEFOLK REALM that they wanted in their wee' Faery Realm; they *could do it*!

Those who chose the PEOPLEFOLK Realm; they were *also free* to openly stay in that Realm! But with the *New Covenant* they gave up the right to be wee' Faeries; use their Faery powers or travel through the Faery Realm. But they *no longer* had *wings* and *no reason* to FLY! They had *happily* chosen 'this way of life' and would live this way; *till the end* of their days!

CONTINUTED ON THE FOLLOWING PAGES

WHAT HAPPENED?

'*AFTER* THE SEVENTH DAY'.......

UPDATE - AFTER THE SEVENTH DAY

****

Prince Davey became a *great KING* – leading his Kingdom into one of the most *peaceful times of existence;* under one rule! His brother Prince Ivan was a *great advisor* for him and helped him immensely in keeping the *peace* surrounding their lands. With Emilie and Rosetta *standing* by their sides; using their Healing 'influential ways' they kept the 'health and the spirit' of Scotland *alive* and *well* while they kept their close *contact* with the 'Invisible Secret Faery Realm'; *a secret!* Queen Ivy also prospered along with her sons and this time round' they *shared* their wealth and helped the *needy* in their *own way*!

Within the Invisible Faery Realm – King William and Queen Isabella were busy with their *families* and *friends* who had gathered around them and who had *chosen* to stay in the wee' Faery Realm!

They all traveled back and forth through the Faery Realm from the Castle Heatheren I *to* the Castle

Heatheren II! Since their Peoplefolk *family* and *friends* could *not come to them* – they could go to visit them in that beautiful room (in the great tower of the Castle Heatheren I); the one which William had made with all those *beautiful* Faery Houses *inside!* The houses were in *all shapes, sizes and colors* surrounded with plants and vegetation and there were even *birds* that flew in and out through the tall Church-like windows through the small openings! It was indeed a HAVEN for the wee' Faeryfolk and *Tom, Roland, Gabriel, Cecile, Nanny Belle* and *Ned;* they all had a HOME set up for the *comfort* and *style* that they loved and could *freely* see one another; whenever they chose! Most of the time; they all *chose* to be at the *Castle Heatheren II*; close to *Isabella* and *William!*

Nanny Belle whose real name, was Louise; *married* that lovely gentleman named Ned Sutherland and they had a *double wedding* - with *Cecile and Gabriel!*

Queen Isabella was *distraught* for she did *end up* getting *very BIG* with child; with *twins* and was not happy to be wearing such a 'large gown' for the occasion! But her Husband; King William loved *all of* _her_; just the same! But she was 'ever _so happy_' for the newlyweds!

Roland had fell in love with Queen Eve, but she would not succumb to _his charms;_ for she was still so much _in love_ with her departed husband, King Roy and it would take her _a long time_ to even think of the _possibility_ of loving _someone else_! She was not lonely for 'company' - for there was _always_ plenty to do! Eve liked being there for her Daughter and loved _helping_ with the preparations for the Healing remedies; which were distributed _secretly_ - with the 'help' of the Healing Faeries in the Peoplefolk Realm! She _was also_ looking forward to _Isabella_ giving birth to _her_ Faery _Grandchildren_!

They _all_ were excited! Her children would indeed _be spoiled_ within the Faery Realm; as Isabella _had been_! They all would see to that!

But ISABELLA had grown _up a lot_ and had turned into a beautiful young woman and an outstanding Healing Faery warrior _and QUEEN_!

Her Mother also knew that _King Roy_ was looking down on all of them and in fact _watched her daily_ from her *night table* - where she *kept the remainder of his ashes*!

Isabella had decided her children would have *lengthy* names for she could not decide; *on just one! Her girl* would be called EVIE HANNAH LOUISE and *her son* would be ROY GABRIEL STEWART; of which *the King* - had *no say*! They all just' *let her be – to be the GYPSY QUEEN*; that she was... People *loved Isabella*; they had *loved her* in the *Peoplefolk Realm* and they loved her *even more* in the *Faery Realm*! They *all* had learnt the IMPORTANCE of 'staying in the moment with one another' and *cherished* each moment of *togetherness*!

They were finally FREE to just BE and there was *nothing pressing* like there had been *before* – it was time to live 'the truth of their trade'; using the *gift'* of the Healing Faeries Creed - to *heal themselves first* and in that HEALING share the LOVE, JOY AND PEACE that came from it and in turn *pass on that GIFT'*...

And as Queen Isabella *said*, "*Never, Never,* give up on your DREAM because the *DREAM* is not only *in* you; *IT IS YOU! NO MATTER HOW LONG IT TAKES, NO MATTER HOW FAR IT TAKES YOU!*

THE END – AND THE *NEW BEGINNING* - *FOR THE HEALING FAERIES!*

THE AUTHOR'S NOTE

****

As life goes on around us; *in our lives*...look around you and know who is standing *beside* you, *behind* you - who is truly you're friend or *who* is a part of your *support system*! Who holds you up when you fall down and who *comforts you* in times *of need*? Is it your fine feathered friends; the animals surrounding you in your life; nature, or the UNIVERSE *itself*? What about *those Healing Faeries* standing right beside us; in *our gardens* watching from the trees - watching over us *forever* and *ever!* This is an *unending* SCOTTISH FAERY TALE; one that shall go on *forever*!

To *catch a glimpse* of the Healing Faeries is *now* only for the EYES of BELIEVERS! The myths, stories and folklore that have been passed on over the centuries; say to *this day*, that 'they still walk among us' doing their *healing work*!

Will they ever return? Have you seen glimpses of them? Do you *believe*? Go out *into nature* and sit for just half an hour' and really look hard and *listen*; not just with your' ears - but with *your heart* and you may feel, see or hear the presense of the HEALING FAERIES CALL and *heed it*! Do something today to create joy, peace and happiness within you and share it with others and you too can pass on the love and *the legacy* of the HEALING FAERIES!

It is *our job* to 'share the story' and keep it going for our children; their children and our grandchildren! It is *our job* to keep the *magic* in their lives and play up' the *magical moments*! Teach them about the <u>importance </u>of 'life's *simple* pleasures' and try to bring *nature* <u>back</u> into their lives; while *we still can*!

Never *dismiss* a child's imagination and the *sheer pleasure* they have in their youth! Let them <u>feel </u>the *joy*, the spontaneity and the *<u>deliciousness</u>* of each *new* day!

Bring back that 'childlike side of ourselves' so we can help each other make *it through* the years to come! Each *one of us* has a part in <u>recreating</u> HEAVEN

ON EARTH; each *one of us* can make a difference, *everyday*!

Play more, love more; don't <u>make</u> life *too serious...* Take a time out of each day to <u>just be</u> and *play* and *smell the roses*! Use your *seven senses!* Fill each day with JOY; like it is your *last.* <u>See, hear and LISTEN</u> to the *beauty* <u>of</u> life! Do not let MATERIAL THINGS or MONEY rule your life so much -you miss all the *child-like wonder* of our HEAVEN ON EARTH! LET our *children* <u>help us</u> bring back the *beauty of; loving life!* Try ever so hard *to* <u>*FOLLOW through*</u> with '*what you SAY <u>you are going to do</u>'! If you keep breaking your promises* to <u>children and others</u> *and* never DO *what you say* you are going to do; *it can ruin your relationships! TRY VERY HARD to watch* <u>*how many times we do this*</u> <u>in a day or a week</u> *and* <u>*try to*</u> <u>*correct it*</u> *– especially when making promises to CHILDREN!!!*

Please help us finish our work! Help us to share our dreams and help others to make their dreams come true! We can do it TOGETHER; no matter what, no matter how long it takes, no matter WHAT great lengths we have to go; just KNOW *we can*!

What I have learnt from writing my Isabella books is; from *BOOK I to BOOK III* – we come *full-circle* with Isabella and like Isabella's *journey* we LEARN that even in the <u>midst of CHAO'S</u>; *miracles* are still happening! You will find that *more love, monies*; even more *opportunities* will come into your lives along with more appreciation of the blessings we *already* have! Sometimes on the OTHER SIDE of that CHAO'S; that's *where* we are *supposed to be*! Sometimes it's our OWN high *expectations* which we put on ourselves that *can sabotage* our own plans! Or if we are pushing *too hard* for something and instead we meet with *resistance*; it may be *because* - there *<u>IS SOMETHING BETTER</u>* coming for us and we just have to be *patient*! It may not be 'WHAT we expected' and *<u>just like Isabella</u>*; it did not turn out how she had planned but 'in the end'; it was the *best* for all of them and gave them the FREEDOM that they desired!

Each one of us is the *<u>Master of our own DESTINY</u>* and we are the *only ones* who can make the <u>changes in our lives</u> that are needed in order to <u>move forward</u> in our lives and <u>only we</u> can *push ourselves* to the *extreme* to *make our DREAMS come true*!

THE GRASS IS NOT GREENER ON THE OTHER SIDE; *JUST MORE GRASS!* **CHERISH the SIMPLE THINGS in LIFE – PLEASE!** *They ARE* **the MOST IMPORTANT.... GOSSIP HURTS; WATCH every word you utter from your 'pretty little mouth' and if you hear GOSSIP/** *STOP* **IT! TRY to** *SMILE* **more; it keeps you younger and** *younger at heart***!**

****

Thank you for coming on this journey with us! I could not have done it without you! *LOVE AND SPARKLES and Faery Blessings* **.......**

Queen Isabella and Nancy Lee Amos

SOME WEE' SCRAPBOOK PICTURES

Like the threads on this <u>patchwork quilt</u> that my MOM made for me; our lives are joined together, our lives intertwined; perhaps <u>passing</u> on the threshold of time! This is a sample of the SIMPLE HOMEMADE gifts' that I talk about in <u>my books</u> that mean so much; an ISABELLA quilt, made by my MOM, with LOVE!

'On the FOLLOWING PAGES are just a <u>few</u> pictures from the <u>Author's own scrapbook</u> and <u>some THANK YOU'S!</u>'

~Thank you for being here with me~

BOOK LAUNCH *for* ISABELLA/
REUNITES THE HEALING FAERIES

These pictures are from the Book Launch from my Isabella BOOK II; Isabella/Reunites the Healing Faeries. It was held in Perth, Ontario at *The Book Nook*! We had it on a lovely March day and had a large turnout! People brought flowers and well wishes and cards and *happily* bought *a lot of books* which *was lovely*!

<u>FROM LEFT TO RIGHT:</u>

*That is me standing in front of the book store; I made sure I had SEVEN brightly colored balloons out front for people to know they had the right spot. (7 being HF's favorite #) I also had on a homemade long blue skirt with *a panel* of 'Issy's/Blue Scottish plaid' in it; with a *blue blouse* and a soft furry navy scarf I used as a shawl. I felt cozy and a bit FAERY-LIKE.*(With wee' small braids in my hair!)

Two people are taking a photo of the DISPLAY window we had showing all the 'artifacts of Isabella's' that go with the books! All the treasures I talk about in the book are actual GIFTS people have given me along the way; which I have <u>incorporated into the stories</u>! All the items talked about in the book; from Isabella's bed made out of 'willow and ash', her Mothers gift of an Amethyst necklace to her *metal* and *wood* chair that is her <u>throne</u>; are in the window! It is fun watching the people look at the display as it captures the hearts' of all ages for everything is on a *SMALL scale* ; FAERY SIZE - which is *so cool*!

*Flowers and gifts given for Isabella and I and *the goodies*; I brought!

*Standing with my Grandson; who came to *see NANNA and Isabella.* (He gets me to TELL him the 3 stories of ISABELLA 'off by heart' <u>without using my books</u>... Since he *is four* I am very animated a*nd he loves it! He <u>can tell me</u>; now!*

*A good friend; with her Grandchildren excitedly waiting for BOOK II...Her granddaughter was in the *drawing contest* I had for the children; using their *own depiction/drawing of ISABELLA!*

*A <u>live radio interview</u> at our local Lake 88 Radio station! (I had to dress the part; I had on <u>my original apron/with Faery Pin!</u>)

There was a great turnout that day and the days following and it always is such a <u>magical time</u> when you get to share <u>your creation</u> with others and the <u>benefits of meeting such lovely children and adults who love the Faeries as much as I!</u> These books are for ages 7 – 97 years of age <u>and UP!</u> Boys and Girls alike; <u>of all ages</u>...

THE ROAD IS NOT LONG;

TO A *FAERY FAITH FRIEND'S* DOOR

This DOOR; yard and garden belong to a friend on P.E.I. – my TEA BUDDY of long ago...and now I have a *new friend* I met here in Perth who is an *Artist* and *who makes* FAERY DOORS and HOUSES! On the following pages you will meet her and see some special' pictures (with special permission of course) of a FAERY HOUSE making workshop; one that *I attended*!

Also I am dedicating these pages to *thanking* once again *other creative talented artists*, friends and family members who have been influential to me and who *inspired me* to move forward in my journey; not only as a writer but *as a friend*!

FAERY HOUSE MAKING WORKSHOP

This was the *most extraordinary* workshop I have ever had the pleasure to partake in! In September I went to CHERYL SINFIELD'S FAERY HOUSE MAKING workshop! I can assure you it was pure 'HEAVEN on EARTH' for me and I am sure for all those *who attended that day*! As you can see in my pictures on opposite page; all the ingredients we USED for our FAERY HOUSES had to be NATURAL and we were supposed to be able to *LEAVE* them in the Faery woods and not leave any synthetic materials or things *man made* behind!

From the *first time* I saw Cheryl's work at our local Holistic shop; called LOTUS WINGS – I knew I HAD TO MEET HER! Someone who was in *our local area* who loved the FAERIES; just as much as I and *I needed to talk with her!* I was excited to share my Isabella books with her and I had to *find out more* - about *HER WORK*!

That day was a glorious sunny day and we all arrived fresh and ready for *an adventure* and Cheryl *did not let us down!* We started off with a 'storytelling time' as we all sat around in a Faery circle; cushioned with 'real beds of different colored mosses! It was beautiful! (We were in the Faery woods that belonged - to a *dear friend of hers!*) Cheryl read us two lovely Faery stories about 'HOW' to build GOOD Faery houses; then when we *were ready* we were asked to go scout and find our SPECIAL SPOT in the woods; one, where *we* thought *would make a good Faery home!* She had lots of supplies there ready for us to use; all natural ingredients and some of us had brought our own special, *meaningful items* that we could leave there, as well! It was *exciting* and *mystical* and *magical* all at the same time! You would swear the Faeries were right beside us guiding us *how* to build them and *where*! We discovered some neat shiny rocks hidden in the woods and an *EMPTY TURTLE shell* was found; by Cheryl's Daughter! These are JUST SOME of the glorious pictures that were taken that day!

ON PREVIOUS PAGE/LEFT TO RIGHT:

*This was how it was when we arrived; a sign was there for Cheryl's Faery Workshops, supplies that we could use to make our houses, large sunflowers, straw, gauze, large pine boughs, sea shells, cedar and *lots of other cool things the Faeries would love*!

*This is Cheryl reading to us and did I forget to MENTION she had on *large beautiful wings* she had made and had brought other 'smaller sized wings' for us to wear and her friend had made us wreaths *for our hair* with streamers; of which - *I wore both*!

*I thought I would show you mine that I made – that is my backpack beside it – I made little steps of rocks leading up to the hole in the rock; and used pine boughs and gauze to camouflage it all! Inside I added rocks/stones from my own Faery garden, *P.E.I. sand, sea shells and herbs from my garden*!

*This is Cheryl's Son – he is actually ON TOP of the LARGE rock where I made my house/he has steps leading up to his Faery Door with *acorns* and bark on his roof! His sister's is amazing also; adorned with a FAERY circle of real sunflowers and a path of sea shells leading to her Faery door!

*I could not help but snap this picture of Cheryl leading off into the woods with her Daughter! How magical! *The last picture* is of Cheryl and her

208

Daughter and I standing excitedly; *feeling elated* to have spent such an amazing time together! It was if TIME had stood still for us that day and a day we would *cherish FOREVER!*

There was about *seven* of us who built Faery Houses that day; but all in all, about ten people were there *for the workshop!* Good food was shared, tea and goodies and oh... *THE FAERIES* were delighted with us for coming *to their woods!* (And a big THANK YOU to our friend who let us make them on her property and with an OPEN INVITATION to come back and *see her* and to *check on* our magical HOUSES anytime of which we MOST CERTAINLY will; especially before the *SNOW COMES!* Thank you Cheryl and *everyone we met* for the most ENCHANTING extraordinary workshop EVER!)

*You will meet CHERYL in the *following pages* and <u>read a message</u> from her; *why* she loves *to work with the FAERIES* within the Faery (REALM) and *why* she has chosen *this form of artwork!*

MY THANK YOU PAGES AHEAD....
ALONG with INFORMATION about
AND thanks to various ARTISTS
FAMILY & FRIENDS

THANK YOU THANK YOU THANK YOU THANK YOU THANK YOU

****

I know I have done some <u>THANK YOU'S </u>in my **BOOK II – Isabella Reunites the Healing Faeries** but with this being *the third* and *final* in my Isabella series this *is my last chance* to say **THANK YOU** and say: **I <u>DID IT! – I DID IT!</u> And I *<u>could NOT </u>*have done it *<u>without YOU</u>! I WISH TO THANK:*

<u>My Mom and Dad</u>; my family members, my three Sisters who have taught me so much and all my nieces and nephews and my Brother who is growing into such a fine Father and outstanding athlete, my Son who I *treasure more everyday* and his family whom *I love*! All my **FAERY FAITH FRIENDS** along the way; those on P.E.I. and in Perth, Ontario where I *presently live*!

<u>My Husband</u> who believed in me and **TOLD ME NEVER TO GIVE UP**/no matter what and his son who I thank for being a *computer wizard*... (To my Husband now I say: **STAY in the NOW and BELIEVE** and have faith that <u>we **ALL**</u> can make a difference in this world and **THAT IS WHAT WE ARE HERE FOR** – lol (So start **TODAY** while we still **CAN!**) He always tells me I am *yelling* when *I capitalize* in typing lol! P.S. Love never dies Willy *<u>it is like the LOCKS of HAIR in my Isabella books!</u>* You have *one more book to read*....to see *the final outcome! My forever love* to Bella and Wallace *our beautiful cats (who are TRUE*

213

FAERY CATS) *who have kept me company* <u>all those</u> <u>hours</u> *typing* and *creating!*

*To Valerie; I forever say THANK YOU for the GIFT OF THE FAERY PIN that started the whole story going! And to 'Gifted Rose' who let me use her place as my haven' while away /whose table I sat and wrote for THREE HOURS writing my whole story line; all the characters names one sunny *MARCH morning!* (WHO is also a Spiritual Guide and does amazing meditation guides and Healing *Dance* classes!)

*<u>My Boss and fellow colleagues</u>/the beautiful *children* I worked with in The LAP PROGRAM/A THERAPUTIC program for children with behavioral problems! THESE books were created *especially for YOU!*

*<u>I would like to</u> *thank Marg Gaiser*: Artist/Painter; who gave me the GIFT of the *<u>Faery Bridge painting</u>* that I used *in my third book!* To <u>all my Nanny</u> <u>families</u> and *<u>their children</u>* who have been a part of this journey with me and who I am indebted to for their inspiration and love; of which (one of their Grandmother's) *is the artist above!* My Nanny Family on PEI where the famous HEALING FAERY GARDEN still remains to this day whom *I think of still;* <u>everyday!</u> By the way two of these families have sets <u>of boys!</u> So boys and girls have followed Isabella and I; *faithfully!*

*<u>Thank YOU...</u> *Arden Belfry*/artist on P.E.I. who created my Isabella designs for me; who now has gone on to be a fine Husband and *Father* and of course, *an outstanding Artist!* She is *beautiful! Thank you!*

*Thank you *my dear new Faery FAITH Friend*; Cheryl Lynn Sinfield: FAERY CE CE Artist/ who designed *William and Gabriel for me for my 3rd book*! YOU ARE SENSATIONAL!

*The *Print Shop /Ottawa/* Thank you, Mike for BOOK I, posters and bookmarks...

*Thank you *Images Inter Alia Print shop* in downtown Perth, Ontario. Thank you Julia; for your 'outstanding work' and your creativity *Mindy*! You have done *amazing work for me*; bookmarks, posters, calendars and also Mindy who co-created my BOOK III cover design and of course helped me get my PERTH *post card venture* off the ground lol...

Thank you, Leslie from The Book Nook; Perth, Ontario for hosting my *Book Launch* at your lovely BOOK SHOP for ISABELLA II and carrying my books and *inspiring me to KEEP GOING*!

Michael From/Book Tales book store on Prince Edward Island for your continued support and till this day; ongoing support selling my books on P.E.I.! THANK YOU!

*THANK YOU *Tish from*; The Irish SCOT-TISH SHOP* /with all her Scottish influence, *support and FRIENDSHIP*!

*Thank you *Cynthia*...MY (inside joke) She is my *TREASURER and ASSISTANT* and *longtime Scottish friend* of Isabella and I; LOL my Faery Faith Friend - from P.E.I.; who *from day one* supported me in my writing my Isabella books! She stayed with me till I finished my manuscript for the *LITERARY*

215

CONTEST on *PRINCE EDWARD ISLAND*; getting our Friend to drive with me; in <u>*a snow storm/blizzard*</u> to make the *deadline date* and get it stamped *before they closed early* due to the snow conditions! But we MADE it and *I did get an award* for the LUCY MAUD MONTGOMERY Children's award! And *again THANK YOU* for *you* and Rosemary sending all those beautiful *SCOTTISH GIFTS* and for *your true healing friendship and for believing* in *ISABELLA AND I* and for all *your heartfelt gifts' & treasures* <u>you *KEEP sending me*</u>! Nan

<u>Thank you my FAITHFUL FOLLOWERS...</u>

I also would like to THANK ALL THOSE WHO BOUGHT MY BOOKS and for all of you who *'believed in me' on this journey* and as with Isabella it is NOT THE END; just a *new beginning*; a clean slate, an empty canvas – *a brand new tomorrow* to create, create, create! Lastly I want to thank *'my publisher's'*; my *production teams* - who have *worked with me* for the sequel of Isabella; <u>one, two and three</u>! YOU are truly amazing; patient and *I thank you*!

THANK YOU, Love and Sparkles, Nancy Lee Amos

'A WEE Bit' of 'info' About the Individual Artists:

(ALSO MESSAGES FROM THEM; TO YOU)

A message from Valerie (Holistic Health Practitioner):

"I want people to BELIEVE in themselves and by using my *various HEALING modalities* I can help *motivate people to do this*! No matter *what your age*; no matter what your *health issues* are – it is *NEVER* too late to *begin*! During this 'healing process' I can help them to BALANCE *body, mind and spirit* while inspiring them to continue *moving forward*; fully *participating* in their *own* HEALING and in their *own lives*! REMEMBER *like Isabella*; keep following your dreams!"

*I also have had the pleasure of working with pet owners using some of my *healing modalities* on their animals. I also have done some 'long distance' healing with people *over the phone* and have continued sending long distance healing on my own afterwards; *with their permission*; of course!
Namaste'
Valerie Farquharson: (Naturotherapist, Practitioner of Reiki, Therapeutic Touch, Energy Balancing, Communication/Well Being/Stress Management, Spiritual Consultant, Certified member of The Academy Of Naturopaths And Naturotherapists)
CONTACT INFO: Email: faeriehealing@hotmail.com

*(This is my friend, who gave me the gift' of the FAERY PIN and many other treasures; over the years – *too many to mention*!) One of the most important gifts'

has been the gift' of her FAERY FAITH FRIENDSHIP over a span of twenty five years! As Valerie calls it on Prince Edward Island – *our Kindred Spirit connection* that has lasted all this time – *our love of the Faeries* and all the different HEALING methods that we have shared' with one another and <u>*we continue to share*</u> and most important like my sisters; *we BELIEVE in one another* and *are inspired by one another* and like 'my MOM' *we cherish* meeting *others* who are <u>*excited about life*</u> and *who BELIEVE in the* magic *of LIFE* ! That *is our life's work* on earth! *Nancy*

A message from Cheryl (Artist) Creator of making / Faery HOUSES & Faery DOORS:

"Faeries are *DEVINE* beings – they are *ANGELS* with the *wings* of Butterflies and Dragonflies... They are here to help our Mother Earth *HEAL* and to protect its animals too! My life's purpose - *through my art*, is to make people *BELIEVE* in the Faeries and other mystical beings; to *give them* more power <u>to do *their* mission!</u>"

*I also had the *pleasure* to create/draw two of Nancy's main male characters* in her book and *brought them to life for her*/The Healing Faeries; *King William* and *Gabriel*! Nancy said they are *true* to their descriptions and *fit perfectly* and that it was 'no accident' that we met and I was able to *create them quickly*; in 'perfect time' for the *action* of her third book! Nancy says THE FAERIES certainly had *lots to do with it* and since *we both; love FAERIES*, <u>*I would have to agree with her*</u>!
Contact: <u>faeriecece@hotmail.com</u>

*(Cheryl has a presence about her that <u>SPEAKS FAERY</u> – she is gentle, loving and kind and her soft spoken voice *soothes you* the minute she talks to you! She is indeed on the right path' for she is an amazing Artist and Faery House and Faery Door *creator* and *decorator*! I have never seen anything so 'raw, so real, honest and *true*' in *her FAERY work* that she does! <u>THANK YOU CHERYL!</u>)*And YES she captured my William and Gabriel <u>*perfectly*</u> in her drawings... they are handsome and have come alive *for me* and now; *for others* who have the chance to MEET them in my books... She captured Gabriel in his rugged stance for he had to work hard for his living and William being close to royalty most of his life is more on the softer' side but do not think he is weak for he is brave and strong too *like Gabriel*! She did an amazing job *drawing them* as did Arden with my *Isabella – she is the perfect Queen of the Healing Faeries*!) Nancy

A message from my Mom; Millie (Artist):

"I would like to <u>*encourage others*</u> to take art classes, take music lessons, learn to sew; whatever it is that *inspires you*; things you have thought of that you would like to TRY; it does not matter *what age you are* or if you *think* it's TOO LATE TO try *something new*! I started *later in life* and I have met so many talented people and have learnt so much *from them*. With Nancy, with her writing her Isabella books; after I read some of her *poems and her story line* I encouraged her to enter her story in the Island Literary Awards Contest and she did and she got an <u>award</u> out of (two hundred people) who entered in the Lucy Maud Montgomery's Children's Award category which inspired her to keep going and *now she has finished BOOK III*! I am very proud of her.

CREATIVITY is like FOOD for the SOUL! Get out there today and try something – it has brought me some very happy memories; many articles in the *newspaper* and 'friendships for a lifetime'! I was also lucky to work alongside *my partner/my Husband* and together we were able to build a successful business out of it and one *that we love!*"

My Mother and Father; Millie and Fred Kikkert have had their own ARTS & CRAFTS business; for over twenty five years! My Father has done the woodworking and my *Mom;* the Tole/painting and together they have had many *craft shows* on Prince Edward Island! Still to this day they are both *busy in their shop* and *art room* getting ready for the *Christmas season!* My mother Millie also *paints* and has had Art shows in various Art Galleries on the Island.

*My Father and Mother have lovingly gone to the *beach for me* and *wrote my name* and *ISABELLA'S* in the sand for my books (for I now live *in Ontario...*) My Mother has helped me in creating Isabella's colors for her hair and her clothes she wears; she made my ISABELLA pillowcase with SWEET DREAMS on it; she drew the Castle Rockland drawing, a wooden sign was made for me; ISABELLA & NANCY'S ROOM (*Dad cut it out) and Mom painted it for me; she made a QUILT for me that you see in book II and III – she also painted the SLEIGH picture and the picture of my GRANDFATHER'S house you see in BOOK III!(Who is not with us anymore...) My Mom has sold a lot of books for me and *both of my parents* have been *very supportive* in my journey of writing my Isabella books...I cannot even think of all the *GIFTS* from the Island I received in the mail to *keep me going* and loving *homemade treasures;* *(My Father also got me my first COMPUTER) which helped in the *creativity* and *writing of Isabella*! CONTACT INFO: You can reach me if interested in their/Prince Edward Island Arts/Crafts; at Email BELOW...

EMAIL: nancythebraveheart@hotmail.com

*IF ANYONE would like to *share any of their FAERY stories* or *pictures* with me EMAIL me/the AUTHOR *at above address*!

*If anyone would like to ORDER any of my ISABELLA BOOKS you can *ORDER ONLINE at this website:* Type in authorhouse.com/then go to (the AuthorHouse official site) and go to bookstore and type in my name!

If you would like to see any of my books; go online and just print in my name Nancy Lee Amos and my books will come up on Amazon.com where you can read *a preview* from *my three Isabella books*! (You can also view my books on AuthorHouse website as well...)

#1 Isabella/ The Secret of the Healing Faeries
#2 Isabella/Reunites the Healing Faeries
#3 Isabella/ Rules Like the Wind

*In *Book I* – you are *introduced* to Princess Isabella and The Healing Faeries and you find out just what *THEIR SECRET IS* and in *Book II* you learn more about the Healing Faeries; their Healing ways, their Faery Creed, their favorite Healing Herbs and Crystal Stones; how Isabella becomes Queen and *what 'DREAM' does Isabella have - for her PEOPLE*? You also see *many photos* of actual Faery gardens in

BOOK II and you come to know the AUTHOR *even more* and *why SHE LOVES Isabella* and the Healing Faeries *so much* and *wants to share them with YOU! There is also a special section in BOOK II – a tribute to the Author's mentor; Lucy Maud Montgomery on the 100th anniversary of Anne of Green Gables!*

*MY *THREE SPECIAL POEMS*....
ABOUT THE AUTHOR PAGE...
(with special PICTURES)

This Poem is for _ISABELLA; from the AUTHOR..._

TRUE BLUE

On that sunny day that you came to me
Upon a whisper _I heard you there_
Like a beacon of LIGHT you _flew_ to me
And sat _upon my shoulder_ while I wrote
You whispered in my _inner ear_
We are the Healing Faeries
We are the ones that sing
We believe in FREEDOM
No harm to anyone
We may be small, we may stay tall
WE may just DISAPPEAR...
But when you need us most
Just know that we are near
We're like the wind, the earth, the sea
Just like the skies above
You will sense that we are there
For you will feel our love
And on that day; before that day was through
I felt a JOY that I had never KNEW
To want something _so much_; to _dream_ about it,
Eat, think and sleep about it
Nothing in my life have I ever given such _ATTENTION_
And such _devotion –_ you have _taught me the meaning_
Of _Loyalty and Emotion_; about _love_ and DEDICATION
And about how to make _our DREAMS COME TRUE_
Now it's TIME to pass this on to someone else
For our time together in the _Peoplefolk Realm_
Is _almost_ coming _to an END_
But we shall _stay close Isabella_
For when you _need me most_
I will be there too

225

You will find me *in my Garden*; where *I shall wait for you*
You will find me - *inside of me; inside of you*
Thank you *my ISABELLA; Queen – thank you* from the *bottom*
Of *my heart* & everywhere else; *in between*
You are my TRUE BLUE believer of a dream; <u>*that did*</u> <u>*come true*</u>!

Love and Sparkles, *Your DEVOTED PEOPLEFOLK FAERY FAITH FRIEND*;
Nancy

FOR ALL THOSE WHO MISS a loved one; who has <u>*passed away*</u> or has been <u>*apart*</u> from someone and *thinks of them still...* I am <u>*dedicating*</u> these TWO POEMS: One that <u>William</u> *wrote for Isabella* and the other; that <u>Isabella</u> *wrote for William...*

****

IN *LOVING MEMORY* to – my Father; Ralph Moore Amos who passed away since starting <u>this JOURNEY</u>! Your LETTERS will be *cherished*; the 'first phone call' and especially *for me* it's your *VOICE* - that I shall always *remember*, your *soft voice*...

YOU CANNOT KNOW THE SPELL YOU CAST
I FEEL THE MAGIC HERE AT LAST
AMONG THE BLUFFS, THE ROCKY SHORES
ONE CANNOT DENY THE SCOTTISH ROAR
OF PRINCESS ISABELLA – THE BRAVEST OF THEM ALL
SPINNING TALES OF HER OWN FOLKLORE
SPINNING TALES OF HEALING HEARTS
SOOTHING GOSSAMER WINGS
FLOATING DOWN TO TOUCH US ALL
WITH, YOU'RE HEALING WAYS...

BREATH THE BREATH OF LIFE SO PURE
FOR IN A MOMENT KNOW FOR SURE
I AM WITH YOU NOW AND YOU WITH ME
NO DISTANCE CAN EVER COME BETWEEN US
NO WATERS EVER TOO WIDE TO KEEP US APART
FOREVER MORE, FOREVER FRIENDS
TILL HEAVEN ABOVE AND THE EARTH WE LOVE,
ARE ONE...

****

Everyone has someone *they miss*...May PEACE and Happiness FOLLOW you all *the rest of your days*... *Nancy & ISABELLA*

'ABOUT THE AUTHOR'

ABOUT THE AUTHOR

Nancy Lee Amos lived on the healing shores of Prince Edward Island for over 'half of her life' – to Nancy it is *her home*! But because of *family ties* Nancy moved to Ontario and now resides in the beautiful Scottish heritage town of Perth, Ontario! The *sister town* to *Perth, Scotland*! Since moving to Ontario Nancy has finished and published her three books on Isabella and the Healing Faeries which she started while *on Prince Edward Island*! Nancy's interest in *children* and the 'healing aspect of life' has lead her to *create* Isabella and the Healing Faeries to help give children and adults *alike* 'hope' and in turn the *faery faith* needed in order to make their *dreams* come true! The *one thing* Nancy has discovered is it's the 'simple things in life' that *heal us* and the universal need to find *peace and happiness* that binds us all! In the first book, <u>*Isabella/The Secret of the Healing Faeries*</u> you are introduced into the life of Isabella who had to do some healing of her own in order to *grow* and be able to help others! In Book II, <u>*Isabella/Reunites the Healing Faeries*</u> Isabella is now able to 'break free' from her past and discovers who *she truly is* and goes on to lead her people showing them new ways to follow their dreams as well as her own! And in the *final book* of the Isabella series; <u>*Isabella/Rules Like the Wind*</u>; Isabella comes <u>full circle</u> and realizes it is her DESTINY and hers alone to '*go to the extreme*' to make her dream come true and through Isabella we all come 'face to face' with the TRUTH that we are the only ones who can <u>make the changes in our lives</u> in order to make our dreams come true – no matter what – no matter how long it takes you – *YOU – ARE THE DREAM*; the dream is *INSIDE YOU*, waiting to *come out*!

THE PICTURES ON PREVIOUS PAGE/LEFT TO RIGHT:

*On the left is a picture of a CASTLE taken many YEARS ago in PERTH, SCOTLAND! A friend of the AUTHORS took a 'braided lock of her hair' to bury by a CASTLE wall! (The uncanny part of this is it was a few years ago *prior* to the beginning of ISABELLA!) And the UNCANNY part NOW is; the AUTHOR *now lives in the sister town of Perth, Scotland – Perth, Ontario!* Also the Lad who buried her hair also put on the back of the photos; "Your hair is buried by the Castle wall along the RIVER TAY - which we also have *a RIVER TAY in Perth, Ontario*! *The Author is seen in one of the pictures with her braids and again she is seen standing along the banks of the RIVER TAY in her new HOMETOWN of PERTH, Ontario! She moved here because of 'Family Ties'!* Talking of FAMILY TIES; there is a picture of *her GRANDFATHER'S house (in which she lived)*; the picture was painted by her Mother and the wee' small picture is the Author *as a baby* with her MOTHER! To the AUTHOR she feels we ALL COME FULL CIRCLE at *one point or another in our lives* and we come to realize we are all connected; in *some way or another*!

230

LOVE and SPARKLES from NANCY and ISABELLA Thank you.......

"I must tell you again that writing my Isabella books; was nothing short of, *'a miracle'* - for it takes *a lot of discipline* and there have *been delays* in the writing of my books; (unforeseen delays) which are *all part of life* and the message I am leaving *in my final book* of the series TELLS YOU that perhaps it was *all meant to be* and the TIMING *perfect*! But this is my GIFT to you; with every new SUNRISE *you DO* get to begin again and again! So it is time that ISABELLA and I leave you and *leave this legacy; this tribute to the Healing Faeries and ALL Faeries and ANGELS of this earth (in the Faery Realm or the Peoplefolk Realm!) Please share our GIFT and your GIFT with others! Do something TODAY to spread this message!*"

****

We shall not say *good-bye* we shall say;
GOOD NIGHT.......

PSssssss... Watch for Faery sightings
AT FIRST LIGHT

And remember *with each new sunrise;
We DO have a chance to begin again*!

"Hear! Hear!" says *Nancy and Isabella*.
"Goodnight; Faery Faith Friends!" they added.
"Till we meet again!" says *Nancy*.